THE ROAD UP AHEAD

THE ROAD UP AHEAD

Short Stories

JONATHAN P. ALCOTT

Raleigh, North Carolina

Published by Clear Sight Books, Raleigh, North Carolina
Cover image by Sherry Cantrell
ISBN paperback: 978-1-945209-18-5
ISBN ebook: 978-1-945209-19-2

This book is dedicated to all those who knew and loved Brian and still miss him to this day.

To my father, William Lawrence, who was a rural mail carrier at the time and suffered with Ralph; to Mary, cloaked in her courage to live each day the best she could; and to all those who have a lost a child.

To my editor, Karin Wiberg, who stuck with me through this story. I've written a lot of stories, but this one was difficult—Brian was my friend.

TABLE OF CONTENTS

THE ROAD UP AHEAD

Mary stretched, still in her flannel pajamas, and looked out the kitchen window right before the term "midmorning" would apply. She lingered thinking about Brian and how best to raise him to be like his father and how to keep him safe. She constantly worried about her ten-year-old—not about anything specific; it was just a general feeling of uneasiness. Her mother would often say, "People who worry needlessly about nothing end up with ulcers." Mary used to think, *How do ulcers know whether it's nothing or not?*

She shivered. She needed to put on warmer clothes. She went to Brian's room to get him out of bed. Another day of no school—the school furnace was on the fritz.

Brian, still half asleep said, "I like fritz," and dozed off again.

Mary had a list of things to do, and the senior high girl

would be here shortly to oversee Brian. The one television channel didn't come on until 10 a.m., and that would be news and livestock reports followed by grain futures, so Brian would do simple math questions and then some coloring. She knew Ralph would think more math or science would be far better than coloring, but he was at work at the post office, so he just didn't have to know.

Outside of schoolwork, Ralph spoiled Brian terribly; nothing was too good for him. This year when Brian had begged his father to go cut a real live Christmas tree, Ralph couldn't say no. He threw an ax in the trunk and off they drove to the country. Mary would have been just as happy to go to a tree lot, but a nice fresh cedar would be lovely. If only it hadn't been so cold. She and Brian had huddled together for warmth while Ralph chopped at the poor tree. He finally hollered, "Tim-ber!" and the tree fell to the snow-covered ground. They'd sung Christmas carols on the way home, and then the real work had begun—getting the tree in the stand.

Mary frowned now looking at the tree. Ralph had tied a piece of twine to the top of the tree and run it to the curtain rod. And another piece ran to a nail that was conveniently sticking out of the door jamb. Oh well. If Brian wanted a fresh tree, she could tolerate a little twine running helter-skelter. At least the rest of the house was decorated festively for the holiday.

MARY GOT HOME FROM HER ERRANDS AND SENT THE high school girl home. "Stay warm!" she said as she waved.

The temperature outside had not risen much from that morning, and there was a strong wind out of the northwest. The radio console in the living room predicted more snow overnight with the temperatures dropping even further.

Brian was playing in the snow outside. Good to have him out of the way while she made Christmas cookies. Every year she baked enough for family, friends, neighbors, and the Christmas party at church. As she worked, she frequently paused to step into the dining room to look out the window to check on him. She noticed that Brian had decided to change his snowman to a snowwoman by placing one of her hats with a veil on its head. She stood in the doorway admiring the beauty of the season. The snow piled up perfectly balanced on the wire clothesline, making a well-defined pyramid. Everywhere she looked she smiled at God's marvelous work to adorn for His creatures a beautiful winter scene.

Large snowflakes slowly started to fall from the gray sky, and Brian began racing around trying to catch them on his tongue.

"Watch where you're running, Brian," Mary called. The large cedar tree in the corner of the backyard was struggling to keep its branches from snapping. With her luck, a branch would land on Brian. "Just a little longer and then it's time to come in!"

Mary heard the timer go off in the kitchen and went back in to take out the cookies and decorate them.

A half hour later, there was a sharp knock on the door. Oh, no. She'd lost track of time. Had something happened to Brian?

She opened the door, and her neighbor was there with Brian.

"I found him on the curb at the bottom of the hill. Looks like he got a little banged up."

Mary could see some scratches on Brian's face and a fat lip. Oh no, what had she done? She felt panic—and justification for all her worrying. Luckily, with her nursing background, she could patch him right up. And with her mothering background, she knew what would really help: hot cocoa.

She thanked the neighbor and took Brian to the kitchen. As he sat eating his cookies and drinking hot cocoa, Mary said, "So tell me, Champ. How'd you get all banged up?"

Apparently, he'd decided to go sledding in the fresh snow, but the yard didn't have enough hills, so he went down the street to a hill that was very steep.

"Didn't I tell you to always let me know where you're going?"

He nodded and continued his tale. The problem with this hill was the road at the bottom. He either had to roll off the speeding sled or ride it across the road and run the risk of getting hit by a car. Mary's eyes widened as he told her how fast he'd gone and his decision to shoot across the road.

"Brian!" she exclaimed. "You could have been killed!"

"Aw, Mom, I looked both ways. And it was really fun to go fast. But I guess that last time I should have rolled off sooner. I couldn't see around a parked car and got stuck under the bumper."

She noticed Brian's cheeks and nose, which had been bright red, were starting to fade.

"Young man," she scolded. "You just wait until your father comes home." Now if only Ralph would actually discipline him instead of spoil him.

SEASON AFTER SEASON CAME AND WENT, ALONG WITH birthdays, school events, ballgames, and trips to relatives; long hot summers accounted for three months out of each year. Brian was now in junior high.

How did he grow up so fast? thought Mary. She knew the other students and the teachers liked Brian, and it must be said that he never got in any serious trouble with authority figures. And yet, here she was still worrying about him.

Brian was a good kid and stayed home for the most part, but he did like to ride his bike around the small town. And she knew that he was sometimes reckless. Neighbors had told her of his riding at high speeds on the sidewalks. But what worried her more was that he was prone to darting out into the street without carefully checking for cars.

Dangerous. That bike is dangerous, she thought. *That boy is a thrill seeker.* How many times had she patched him up? Most recently he'd collided with another boy who was on his bicycle; Brian was going fast and crossed in front of him, hooking his back tire on the other boy's front tire. They both lost their balance and fell hard on the road. Brian was scraped up pretty good. *Maybe that's why my mother suggested I be a nurse—she knew I'd have a daredevil child.*

The phone rang, and Mary grabbed the receiver. The operator made sure it was Mary before connecting the two parties.

"Hello, hello?" It was the hospital. "Oh, yes, I'll come on in as soon as I can."

Mary sat Brian down and told him that she expected him to do exactly as she instructed while she was gone.

"And if you're good—no bike today—maybe we'll go to the drugstore for a limeade."

In late 1959, Brian met the legal requirements to drive on the roadways of Missouri. Mary was not pleased with this big step. Honestly, she thought some level of protection was lost. She knew how fast Brian liked to go on his bike, and she'd heard that when he was a student driver, he'd pushed the limits with his instructor. He was always polite around adults, including her, but she knew he could talk his way out of anything. He was hard to resist—always joking and having a good time, he had a charismatic personality. She and Ralph had indulged him more than they should have. Lord only knew what he did when there was no adult around.

He was a teenager. He was growing up, and regardless of her warnings and worries, he would do what he wanted to do. But she refused to let him take the car with his girlfriend, Beth. He would just have to keep going on double dates to the VFW ice cream socials or school band concerts or the movies.

It was a beautiful October day—crisp air in the morning and not a rain cloud to be seen. Brian was fifteen and a few days and wanted to go for a ride with his cousin Mack to help celebrate this rite of passage. Ralph had given in to

Brian's request, and Mary was worried sick at her stomach. Ralph. Why had he done that? And now he was at work at the post office, staffing the counter. It was Saturday, which meant a lot of farmers would come in to buy stamps and mail packages. For some reason he liked working Saturdays and liked being on hand when the rural mail carriers returned from their routes. But that meant Mary was left to worry alone.

She'd spent so much time worrying about Brian over the years. More than once she'd wondered if Brian sensed her constant concern. She'd been preoccupied when he left that morning, and she hadn't reminded him to be careful. Her worry would continue until he walked back through the door. *Joy ride*, she thought. *It is no joy for me. Driving fast with the windows down, no doubt.* Speed was his thrill. She and Ralph had warned him about the dangers of speeding, but he loved to live on the edge, and consequences didn't seem to matter. *That boy has a false sense of security.*

Then she remembered something her mother had said: "Worry is a lot like a rocking chair—they both occupy your time, but they don't get you anywhere." Well, at least they were both soothing. And she had a flyer to work on for the PTA—that would keep her mind occupied for a while.

THE PHONE RANG, STARTLING MARY OUT OF HER FOCUS on the PTA project.

"Hello?"

"Hi, Mary. This is June at the police department. There's been a car accident and the coroner isn't available, but he suggested that since you're a registered nurse you could go to the scene to pronounce death and then later you could fill out the paperwork together. Would you be able to help? It's out on Highway 123 just in Polk County. You know, that curve where Sylas's Oldsmobile spun out a couple months back."

"Yes, if you can send an officer to pick me up, I'll come out."

THE POLICE OFFICER PULLED UP TO THE SCENE OF THE accident. There were several spectators, but they kept a respectful distance from the area the police had roped off. The car appeared to have rolled and was in the field, its underbelly facing the road.

"Over here, ma'am. It appears the driver was ejected from the car. He landed over here in the grass. We still haven't identified the body."

Mary walked briskly after the officer. She was here to deal with a serious matter; she needed to be at her best and represent the hospital well. But she had to admit this was not a job duty she wanted to retain.

The officer gently rolled the body over.

Mary sank to her knees. *No!*

Later, the death certificate would say Brian's death was due to severe head trauma. The certificate also noted, "Death was instant."

MARY WAS IN SHOCK, NUMB. IT WAS THE MOST HORRIBLE day of her life. She tried to cry, but nothing happened.

She had no physical or mental sensation. She couldn't breathe. *How could God have done this to us?* And it didn't get any better . . .

In the aftermath of the accident, she knew Ralph was suffering too, but she could be no help to him. She could only go to the door of Brian's bedroom and look at his bed that he'd made with his two hands that fateful October morning. He would never sleep in that bed again or make up that bed again. Again, and again, she said to herself, "I want to die."

ONCE MACK GOT OUT OF THE HOSPITAL, HE CAME TO see Mary.

"We were having so much fun, Aunt Mary. The windows were down, and I could feel the wind in my hair. We were just *happy*, and we kept laughing at everything. We even honked at a dog. But Brian kept going faster and faster—you know how he is . . . was. He asked me if I was nervous, and I should have said yes, but I didn't want him to think I was a fraidy-cat. He kept looking at me with that face he would make when he was in trouble—or talking himself out of it."

As Mary sat and listened, she did her best to look calm and collected, but the shattered look on her face said it all.

"Then we got to that winding part of the road and I was going to tell him to slow down but then—I don't know what happened—the car fishtailed and then tilted and suddenly everything was confused. I guess that's when the car was flipping, but I think I lost consciousness. When I came to, all I could hear was the sloshing of the radiator water and gasoline. And I couldn't see Brian."

Mack started crying.

Mary hugged him and felt guilty that she resented having to comfort the one person who could have stopped Brian from dying that day. "Mack, Brian was driving way too fast. Even an experienced driver couldn't have managed that curve. I just wish he would have listened to me and stopped going at such a breakneck speed all the time."

Mack sniffed and nodded. After a moment, he asked, "How's Uncle Ralph?"

Mary couldn't answer. When Ralph had received the news, he was upset to the point of a nervous breakdown. He was currently in a mental institution; there was even discussion of shock treatments. Mary could barely hold herself together; dealing with her husband's state was about to push her over the edge. Friends and relatives were taking shifts around the clock, staying with her to make sure she would eat and sleep and not do anything drastic.

THE WINTER MONTHS WERE FILLED WITH DARK GRAY days and cold black nights. The trees without their leaves were like skeletons, gloomy skies mixed with a wet chill, the grasses were dead, and the dying season beckoned only loneliness.

Ralph was now home and had returned to work, but he was a man going through the motions. Like Mary, he was void of personality and life, just trying to make it through each day. All Mary could do was pray, asking how she could have prevented this horrible event from ever happening and begging for healing. The only relief Mary found was at bedtime, which came early in the hopes that sleep could suffocate her terrible pain and emptiness, and by which time she was exhausted.

As a medical professional, she knew that exhaustion was nature's way of slowing the body and mind so that healing could occur, but that knowledge didn't help. She was often restless and walked the same path through the small home over and over, never really tiring of it, just walking without speaking.

She finally accepted the pain and let it settle in. And she recalled something else her mother used to say: "The same fire that hardens steel also turns glass into art."

✦

THE DIAMOND BROKER

GAYE SAT NEXT TO THE COZY FIREPLACE THAT her dad had designed specifically for the family's mountain home. He was proud of the fireplace and the home. The logs had finally caught hold and were putting out enough warmth to heat the entire house. Gaye was wearing her favorite heavy wool sweater and denim jeans. In addition, the wool lap blanket was great for pulling up to her chin to ward off the below-freezing temperatures outside.

Until six months ago the mountain home had belonged to her father, Dean Parker. When he passed away unexpectedly, Gaye had been the sole heir, inheriting what was now her favorite place. She was based in Los Angeles and lived in an older refurbished apartment complex on the corner of Sixth and Vermont, but the chance to go to Montana at times was a lifesaver. As a diamond broker, she traveled to shows regularly. The company she'd worked for the past seven years was Five Star Diamond Brokers. Her responsibilities required her to conduct shows for major retail jewelry stores around the country. In addition to the shows, she was responsible for the diamonds themselves. She liked the glamour of her job, but occasionally she needed a break from the high-pressure world. And over the past year there had been five diamond robberies. Gaye was determined that she was going to catch the crooks—they had profited off the diamond business long enough. No doubt this would help her secure the promotion she wanted to directorship of the Northwest territory. But the stress of the job and the needed vigilance sometimes fatigued her.

The cabin sat at the base of the Bridger Mountain Range in Bozeman, Montana. This was where the family would come every December. It was where they reconnected, where news was exchanged, family dinners were shared, and photos were taken to update their albums.

Sadly, interest in the family's cabin had begun to decline when Gaye's mother died. Then her older brother Robert, who had bouts of depression and was moody most of the time, walked out the door one Thanksgiving Day, severing ties with the family. The bird remained uncarved, and the mashed potatoes became a solid cold clump. Everyone had lost their appetite.

That particular holiday was a waste, a reminder of how the family was slowly crumbling. Now, Gaye clung to the knowledge that her dad had loved her. She felt special because her dad had woven his name in with hers, Gaye Deana Parker.

She looked out the window and enjoyed the huge snowflakes floating to the ground. Bing Crosby's song "White Christmas" was grinding out over and over because the mechanical record exchanger had failed to switch to a new record. For a moment, Gaye felt a little melancholy and lonely. Given her strength, she quickly shook off such silly emotional stuff and thought about how Daddy—a term she often used when she was feeling down—had raised her to be tough and resilient, something he could never accomplish with Robert.

Her boyfriend, Charlie, was supposed to have joined her the day before, but he'd bowed out saying he was too busy to take time off. His change of heart coincided with the onset of a heavy snowfall. This wasn't the first time he had shown his true colors. She remembered six months earlier when he was supposed to go on a float trip down a Class V river nicknamed "The Skull." He made a flimsy health excuse, but in everyday language his reason was "chicken."

She thought, *There's something not right with him.* Even when he was there with her physically, his mind seemed to be somewhere else.

She had dated Charlie Whitehead for the past year. She was in her mid-forties, and Charlie was ten years her junior. The age difference didn't bother her, but she imagined it made Charlie feel more mature. She was tall and slender, with natural blond hair, big blue eyes, and a million-dollar smile that seemed to go well with her job, where she met many rich clients. She knew she could turn the head of any man, and she knew Charlie liked that. But she also knew her confidence radiated to the point that many men were intimidated by her. With her blond hair and rosy-red lips, when she dressed in all black, she was the perfect representative to be hosting a diamond show. The wealthy clientele loved her, and just maybe sales were a little easier to come by.

Her personality was captivating—and threatening to those who were weak in their skin. She was beginning to suspect that might be the case with Charlie. *He's got no spunk. I wonder if he knows what living is about.* It might be time to get rid of ole Charlie the way she had her husband.

GAYE ARRIVED AT THE DALLAS/FORT WORTH AIRPORT where she was shuttled to Black Acres, the hotel where the jewelry show would be held the next day. There she met the three major jewelry store owners who would be the main clients of the show. The diamonds were always sent out to her next appointment ahead of her arrival and were always accompanied by two company guards, so her first job was to verify the merchandise had arrived and was secured and to notify her company that all was well. When the show was finished, an armored service would pick up the merchandise and ship it back, relieving Gaye of the pressure and worry that comes with millions of dollars in diamonds. This show was a little different from past shows. Most of the time shows were held at a hotel in a large banquet room. However, this show was taking place in a jewelry store, the largest serving Fort Worth and Dallas, home to the oil barons.

The jewelry store owner, Jack Wells (the story goes that he had so many oil wells he had changed his name to Wells), owned the largest store in the area and hinted that he was interested in making a sizeable purchase. It didn't take long to notice that Jack had interests in things other than diamonds: every time he passed, he would brush up against Gaye, making sure his hand found her rear or thigh.

Gaye decided Jack needed to be put in his rich place. The next time he did it she said, "Jack, I always thought Texas was a big, big state, and yet you seem to always brush against my ass when you walk by." When she had finished scuffing Jack's shine, she rested her hand on his shoulder, leaned in close, and whispered a conciliatory comment about not offending him while at the same time depositing a nice blond telltale strand of hair for Mrs. Wells to find. She gave Jack a long, friendly smile and slowly walked away.

Gaye was respected in the industry, but that didn't preclude these rich guys from trying to get her alone on their yachts in the Mediterranean or their penthouses in New York. With her big smile she would compliment them on their exquisite taste in jewelry, and now in women, and would give them a playful but firm no.

At packing up time, Gaye was boxing up the last small felt-lined display box when the armored guards walked in with their canvas bags for toting the bulk of the diamonds to the truck. She noticed that one of the men seemed a little out of place with the other two and also with her experience of guards in the past. He came across as jumpy, looking around like he was watching for cues or directions.

Gaye moved to the front of the store where she could see the truck. She carefully scanned it, looking for anything out of the ordinary. Just as she was about to turn and walk back to the center of the store, she noticed the armored services sign was crooked. *How strange is that?* she thought.

She went to the glass front doors, looked from that angle and was even more mystified by the sign. *It's like the whole sign is tilted.* She walked over to the guards and said, "They're sending up some new paperwork. You'll need to wait a minute."

One of the guards became irritated.

She snapped, "Is there a problem?"

He quickly settled down and shook his head.

Gaye walked over to the house guard and firmly instructed him to call the Dallas police immediately. "And don't act any differently."

Within seconds the entire block was full of police cars. Three officers in riot gear came up to the front doors, and four surrounded the armored truck. Gaye exited the building and escorted a policeman to the crooked sign. It was a magnetic sign, temporary at best. The policeman pulled it off the truck; underneath it read Inter-City Armored. Two more officers joined the four guards. They started pounding on the doors and finally the men start filing out: three men dressed in beach attire, unshaven and looking like they had just woken up. One of the police officers leaned over and said to another officer standing nearby, "They're never as smart as they think!"

The store manager approached Gaye and congratulated

her on her fine detective work. The two of them answered question after question from the police. One of the detectives confided in Gaye that there was some kind of inside work in this attempted heist. "We don't have any more than that at this time, but we'll get there. That's for sure."

During the ride back to the airport Gaye thought, *Inside job, hmm. Well, at least gropy Jack Wells bought something.* But the whole flight time back to L.A. all she could think about was the inside heist.

The next morning Gaye was greeted with a lot of fanfare and a hint at a raise, but later when alone with the managing director, she indicated that she would much prefer the promotion to the Northwest over any monetary compensation. After her request, he raised his eyebrows and held them as if to say, "Look, I'm thinking about your preference." At any rate, Gaye was too much of a professional to get wrapped up in body language.

THE PLANE LANDED AT LAGUARDIA, WHERE GAYE WAS met with a security detail arranged by Five Star Diamond Brokers. From there, she was chauffeured to the Waldorf Astoria. Normally she would arrive at the banquet room at 8 a.m. the next day, but during these most cautious times, she was going to visit the layout that evening. She carried her legally licensed 38mm revolver, just in case. Her company required her to be trained in how to use the gun, including safety, due to her job.

As she stepped off the elevator, she moved with awareness of who was close by. Once in the large room where the merchants would be, she asked a bellman to bring Mr. Porter, the banquet manager, to her. He quickly said no, no it wasn't necessary to call a porter. At first, she was confused, but then figured out the bellman was confused. With some patience she got it all straightened out with him, and then up walked Mr. Porter. In the end she muttered to herself, "Well, I'll be."

After a cordial greeting, they retired to his office to go over the plans for transporting the diamonds. Gaye took charge of the meeting and asked to see the corridor where the diamonds would travel.

She pointed out where she wanted armed guards stationed along the corridor from the safe to the conference room. She was quick to point out to Mr. Porter that her company would pay the cost of the extra guards.

"Now, Mr. Porter, you and I are going to walk the very path that the diamonds will travel."

She saw Mr. Porter had not yet fully grasped the gravity of this practice run. She stepped out in front of Mr. Porter, causing him to stop in his tracks. With her hand at about his chest height, she had him frozen like a crossing guard. "Mr. Porter, are you tired of this or what?" *Take it easy, Gaye,* she thought to herself. "Mr. Porter, I mean we're going to walk from the front door of the safe."

"Oh," he said. "Well, let's step back in this room and I'll have the electric panel slid out of your way."

As they stood facing a wall in his office, with the gentle purr of a motor, one half of the wall swallowed up the other half, and there stood the big safe. It was black with gold lettering that spelled the name BUTTERFIELD SAFE CO and had a chrome combination knob.

Not cheap, Gaye thought.

"It sure looks impressive," she said. Again, she held up that commanding hand to tell Mr. Porter it would not be necessary to open the safe.

She backed up to the safe with her derriere touching the door and told him to lead her on the very same route the diamonds would travel in the morning. She followed him, taking precise one-foot steps that she had practiced. She timed the elevator ride and made notes of the whole trip. She thought, *This is pretty simple and straightforward. Now the diamonds need careful watching.*

Back in her room she tried to call Charlie. Still no answer. She wasn't worried, but she was confused. *Where can he be? This is very strange! I'll be!*

The phone rang, waking her up. She checked the clock: 3 a.m. Hesitantly, she answered the phone. "Hello? Who is calling?" No answer. "Hello? I say, who is calling?" Still no answer. She was starting to wonder why these types of calls always seemed to happen when she was out of town at a show.

She jumped to her feet and had the hotel get a hold of Mr. Porter. While she was waiting, she threw on a pair of black slacks and a white silk blouse with tiny gold metal buttons. Quickly but effectively, she ran a brush through her hair. The phone rang, and she grabbed it before the second ring could sound.

"Hello?" she said, sounding slightly out of breath. "Mr.

Porter, I need for you to meet me at the safe area with an armed guard. I'll explain then. See you in ten."

She hung up the phone and left the room. Luckily, the elevator took her straight to the ground floor. The ride gave her just enough time to put on her lipstick, using the gold plate that surrounded the elevator buttons as a mirror.

"Perfect," she said as the doors opened. There with a guard stood Mr. Porter.

She started telling him about the phone call, but it was more than that—it involved the other attempted heist. As Mr. Porter got his information sheets together, Gaye stood patiently thinking about piecing together the mystery of the diamond thefts. Her main interest was stopping the thieves but it wouldn't hurt to help earn a promotion to directorship of the Northwest territory so she could essentially live in Bozeman year-round.

"Porter, in your opinion, does everything look secure here?" she asked.

"Yes," he replied.

She said, "I'm going to contact my company's security group and make arrangements for a security detail to be here. Porter, do you have a problem with that?"

"No," he quickly answered.

"Good," she said. "It's all set then."

THE DIAMOND SHOW WAS A BIG SUCCESS AND EVEN GAYE found herself aware that she couldn't come up with a valid criticism.

She watched the guards carefully as they organized the

locked canvas bags of diamonds, and she watched as they went down the hall. Her eyes enlarged to catch what she was seeing. One guard walked past the janitor's room. As he got to the door, he changed hands holding the bag he carried; he set the bag down for a moment, and the closet door opened, blocking her view. Then he straightened up, again holding the bag. It looked identical to the all the others—no obvious switching of bags. And that's when it clicked with Gaye. A switch—or was there?

She dashed down the hall, shouting at the guard to stop and calling for Porter to bring a diamond company guard. Eventually, the guard stopped, looking shocked at the uproar.

"What's this all about?" he asked.

Gaye said, "Open the bag."

"Well, if you say so," he said.

As the guard opened the bag, Gaye kept thinking about the old trick "Where's the pea?"

Gaye took the open bag and with her jeweler's loupe began to carefully examine the diamonds. When she'd inspected almost all of them, she gazed at the floor while she thought things through. The look of puzzlement disappeared from her face and a smile broke out in its place. She told the company guard to arrest the man who had been carrying the bag.

Gaye explained what had almost happened. The guard carrying the diamonds knew he was being watched closely. His plan was to set the bag of diamonds down and switch that bag for an empty bag; all of this was supposed to happen when the closet door was wide open concealing the switch.

Then he would have proceeded on down the hall as though everything were fine.

Gaye stepped into the janitor's closet looking all around—under a mop sink, behind some broom and mop handles. Then she glanced up at the tile ceiling. She took a broom and poked the ceiling tiles up one at a time. When she poked the last one, down fell a fine soft leather bag containing nice casual men's clothes inside all neatly folded up with instructions where to meet later the next day.

After that episode, Gaye lobbied hard to switch to the company's security team exclusively. She drove her point home: "While I'm good—I can see a crime brewing—one day I will miss it, and the cost of insurance premiums will more than exceed the extra cost of the company security."

The next week Gaye received the promotion to the Northwest she'd been hoping for. Her first act as director was to institute the full use of the company's security team at major shows. Her second act was to dump Charlie. Her third act and most important decision was to book a flight to her cabin in Montana.

✦

DEATH AND RICHES

ELMER AND CLEADETH HAD BEEN FRIENDS SINCE they were little boys. Elmer was the shorter and more agile and the one who had the most courage. He didn't seem to be afraid of doing or trying anything; some people thought he would end up breaking his neck. Most of all, good looks had not been kind to him. He was missing two teeth, one on top and one on bottom, and blocking the looks of that out of your mind, well, he was just downright ugly. He told Clea one time that his mother wouldn't nurse him when he was a baby. He said she told him that she wanted to be his friend and not someone like a milking cow. It was then that Clea mumbled a little too loudly under his breath because Elmer heard him plain as day, "That was because you were so darn ugly."

Cleadeth, on the other hand, was the studious one; he would become remorseful if he didn't get a hundred percent on every test he took. When Cleadeth was cleaned up with his hair slicked back he had a striking appearance—not handsome, not ugly, but somewhere in between. In 1914, the two were boys growing up in a world where few conveniences were enjoyed. The little town they came from was called Foxwood. Both of their daddies were farmers of rough, unproductive soil—or at least they thought it was unproductive, according to the agriculture teacher at the four-room school they attended.

Their friendship continued through WWI when they were stationed together in Germany. Many times they discussed big plans about what they would do when the war was over, if they were still alive. They thought horse breeding would be a good respectable business to own, though they were not bashful to admit that they didn't have an in-depth understanding of how it all worked. Oh, they knew that a mare and stallion had to get friendly, but the idea of bloodlines left them in a pile of unmanageable confusion, searching for relief from the suffering of trying to figure things out. Finally, they decided it was beyond them and they gave up on the idea. What would they do instead?

Eventually both Elmer and Cleadeth were dishonorably discharged from the army. According to them, it was for petty stuff, but later it was learned that these petty charges were in fact considered serious. Thievery, plain thievery. They lived their lives then as they had always lived: if you wanted something and couldn't afford it, then the only other reasonable option was to just help yourself. Two officers wanted to shoot them, but that was ruled out as being a little barbaric for the civilized United States Armed Services.

It was late one cold evening when the two were huddled around an old potbelly stove high up in the mountains of the Continental Divide. They had just finished tugging away on some tough leathery flank steak they'd cut off an elk that appeared to have fallen from a bluff and broken its neck. They didn't care how they came by their dinner—it tasted good and that was all they wanted at the moment.

"Elmer," said Clea, "let's work hard at becoming very rich!"

"I'm with you, old friend. Riches is our goal. Riches is our only goal!"

They hunted and trapped for rare pelts, which included stealing snagged critters from other trappers' catches. They sold just enough to buy a little bit of salt pork, beans, and a slab or two of bacon, but most of the money went to buying several jugs of rye whiskey. Eggs were no problem—stealing them was easy and the farmers generally blamed it on foxes, snakes, and even a badger if they were really dumb. All in all, they ate very well for two grown, healthy men who hadn't lifted a finger in some time.

They reaffirmed their long-term goals one evening when the whiskey had warmed them up real good and their shirt sleeves revealed the grease stains of a king's meal.

"No napkin is ever needed," said Elmer.

Cleadeth, the more fastidious of the two said, "You know, Elmer, one of these days we need to wash our clothes. And a good lathering of our bodies would be nice too. Now, don't go getting angry, but I do believe that you're starting to smell a little ripe."

"Well," said Elmer, "I think you may be right." After a very long pause, he said, "Tomorrow, if it's a warm day, I'm taking my clothes and body to the river."

"Now don't go taking offense and doing something you'll regret later. I was just saying out loud," said Cleadeth.

Elmer said right back, "No, I know when there's stink around, and I've been smelling something too, you know. I'm not dumb to foul air. Clea, I want you to know that I pride myself on two things, and that's 'stink' and 'ugly.'" He added, "I'm sure glad that we've got that ugly part licked."

They both laughed and laughed.

They spent the next day talking about their future and how they could become respectable citizens of the community. They got excited when one of them brought up the idea of being undertakers. All they needed was two black suits and learning to look sad and depressed.

"The looking sad and depressed part is easy—that's about the way we are every day."

"Yeah, but the two black suits will be really hard to come by."

As luck would have it, they came by a bolt of black broadcloth perfect for a suit. They traded a tailoring lady some labor and handyman work for her skills, and in no time, they had two very nice suits—without pockets because that cost too much money.

Clea said, "It's not the best sartorial display of thread and needlecraft, but it'll do."

"We need a parlor to lay out the stiffs if the family is against having the stiff in their parlor," said Elmer.

"Elmer, you can't be calling the dead 'stiffs.' We need to learn to be sympathetic, mournful, and caring. You know, we need to look sorrowful like we lost someone too."

"Well, heck, I can do that if that's all that's worrying you. I can't believe that you've missed the sensitive side of me, Clea." Elmer lifted his knee up and smacked it with his palm and said, "It's a deal. We are now officially undertakers ready to help pass the dead from this world on into the next world."

Clea stood with his mouth open in amazement that such beautiful words were uttered by ole Elmer.

The two pooled their money from selling pelts and picking up tips in the bar and rented a small house with a parlor that would serve nicely as the room for displaying the body.

The very next day a knock came at the front door. Cleadeth, dressed in his black suit, opened the door slowly in a very somber way to illustrate that they were already very sorrowful.

"Hello, ma'am. Would you please step into our lovely parlor?" The room was artistically set with the correct mood lighting—not by design, but because they couldn't find another lamp.

Once they were seated, the lady spoke first. "I'm Mrs. Dixon, and my husband passed to the other side," at which point she glanced up and to her right signifying a spiritual transportation to the heavens.

Without thinking, Cleadeth slowly and reverently followed her gaze until he caught himself. Awkwardly he said, "I know this is a difficult time, and we're here to help ease your burden."

"No," she said. "It is I who will ease your burdens. I know you and your partner don't have a pot to p—"

And it was here that Cleadeth was able to stop her while she hesitated to use such a vulgar word. Cleadeth, feeling a bit smug that he was able to cast aspersion by being the one above such vulgar and unholy words, gave her a tiny sardonic smile, just enough to let her know that she wasn't dealing with someone who couldn't afford pockets in his suit. "Please explain such a statement, Mrs. Dixon."

"Well, as I was about to say, I know that money is an item in the chain of assets that has escaped you two."

"So?"

"'So,' you say in a very flippant and cavalier way. Sir, please tell me how you intend to stay in business where there are no assets—not even a paltry petty cash fund."

"Mrs. Dixon, I'm a very busy man, and I would appreciate it if you would get to the point taking the shortest possible thoroughfare."

"All right, sir, here you are as straight outright as any lady such as I can be. You two have messed with the neighbor's sheep all your lives."

She looked at him with a *malocchio* stare that scared him to the point he was afraid his tricky bladder might let go.

"Now you two scoundrels would sell a widow woman a two-pant suit and not have one minute of regret or guilty feelings. Feelings? That's a funny word to use with you two."

Quietness settled over the room. Cleadeth was so nervous he continued to stretch his legs out and then pull them back in again.

Finally, he said, "I must ask you straight out: do you want us to provide the services for your husband or not? Yes or no?"

"I'll pay you two thousand dollars for a pauper's grave."

"I don't understand. That kind of money is far from being a pauper's grave."

When she didn't answer, Cleadeth, losing his diplomatic behavior a bit said, "Lady, I'm about done with you, so speak up or—"

Before he could finish, she said, "I killed my husband."

When Clea heard that he practically fell out of his chair. Leaving Cleadeth in his turmoil, Mrs. Dixon slipped out the front door. But as she was leaving, she turned around and said to Cleadeth, "Honey, don't just stand there with your mouth hanging open. Something is going to take up residence in there."

All Clea could say was "Weird."

A FEW DAYS LATER MRS. DIXON RETURNED WITH AN even more unbelievable offer, four thousand dollars and a nearly new funeral carriage and horse. Cleadeth and Elmer could barely contain themselves until she left.

Then came a round of boyish shoulder slugs born out of wild excitement.

Clea was the first to speak, "I told you we would make money one day! Lo and behold that day is upon us!"

The next day Mrs. Dixon pulled up in her old Model T. She opened the door, and with the motor still running, she waved the boys out.

Elmer and Cleadeth peered into the back seat. There was Mr. Dixon, who looked like a trussed-up holiday turkey.

"Get him inside and I'll pay off my part of the deal. Any minute the wagon will pull up."

No sooner were the words spoken than there came the wagon and horse. Both Elmer's and Cleadeth's eyes bugged out at what they saw.

Elmer said, "That horse needs to be in the back of the wagon! He's dead—he just hasn't taken the time to fall over yet!" The poor horse's belly looked to be just inches from dragging on the ground.

"Ma'am, if I may say, some of these requests are a tad bit beneath us. We are put in a compromising position when it comes to sleeping with dignity each night."

Mrs. Dixon replied, "You two don't even know the word 'dignity,' other than it is used to degrade you simpletons."

At these disparaging words, the two men stiffened like the corpse in the automobile. Nonetheless they held out their hands for the money, and then hauled the body inside.

As Mrs. Dixon was about to leave, she turned towards Elmer and said, "I don't want to know where my husband's body is buried or anything about this whole ordeal." She turned and looked down the road, and using her index finger as a pointer with the dexterity of a schoolmarm using a wooden stick on the blackboard, she began a list of dos and don'ts.

Her seriousness didn't go unnoticed by Elmer. He also noticed the arthritic finger that still toted heavy jewelry.

She went on for some time about washing her hands of this mess. At long last she became terse and, with a concluding tone, said, "When you see my license plate roll out of sight, that is just the way I am with this mess." She added, "You boys just haven't had a nice dalliance with a fine lady."

Elmer leaned in close to Clea and asked, "Will penicillin cure that?"

Clea leaned back trying to get a good look at Elmer and figure out whether he was kidding or not.

TWO WEEKS LATER, THE TWO PROFESSIONAL UNDERtakers were considering the outlook for their business and debating how likely the chances were that they would remain in business. After all, Mrs. Dixon had been a fluke in several ways. Honestly, how many wives could they expect to waltz in with their dead husbands whom they'd murdered?

Elmer, with a brilliant, excited look said, "Let's sell the business!"

Cleadeth, who had become agitated over the past few days shot back, "Listen, you ragamuffin. What would we sell? The horse? We'd need to prop him up! How about the files containing our sales? We can always tell the buyer that the one stiff—and I do mean stiff—we had we dumped in a dry riverbed. Honestly, we should get out of town while the getting is good."

Elmer began to object, but Clea quieted him. "Shush! I heard something."

There was a sound of knuckles rapping on the door.

"I recognize that knock." He approached the door with caution, fearful of who might be on the other side. Slowly he opened the door barely a sliver, just enough to peek at the person with the audacity to return.

A voice came roaring through the sliver. "Let me in, you two scoundrels; I'm going to kick some behinds when I get in there!"

Elmer came rushing over to the pending crisis. "Why, it's that crazy Mrs. Dixon, isn't it?"

Cleadeth nodded.

Clea opened the door and there stood the squatty Mrs. Dixon in a cloud of perfume, looking like she was out for blood. Every finger, even her thumbs, was laced with rings—rings with rubies, emeralds, diamonds, and jade.

Clea was out of diplomacy, his funeral-home manners long gone. "What do you want?"

Mrs. Dixon barged in and saw Elmer off to one side. "You little pipsqueak! Get over here next to your partner in crime. We've got some jawboning to do. Where is my husband buried?"

"Well, it's like this . . ." Cleadeth started. "We've had a lot of rain, so he could be out to sea by now."

"What do you mean by that statement?"

"Lady, you said to give him a pauper's grave, so we buried him in a dry riverbed, and, well, you can imagine the outcome with all the rains we've had . . ."

"You two aren't fit to be milking a bull. You're numbskulls!"

"No, lady, you're the numbskull—you can't milk a bull!"

With that comment, she jumped up huffing and puffing. She grabbed her handbag, clutched her jacket, and stormed towards the front door.

"Mrs. Dixon," Clea said, "let's call the police and get this settled."

She stopped dead in her tracks at the word 'police.' Slowly, she turned facing her enemies and said, "You know the police can't be brought in for this matter." Her face got red. "Okay, what do you two want from me?"

Elmer said, "We want to be left alone."

She stepped back and took a deep breath, filling her lungs and, naturally, heaving her bosom. It didn't take much to notice four eyeballs staring at her blouse area. Notwithstanding the rugged nature of these two men who had traveled the streets of Paris and its friendly and welcoming brothels, she was ready to bring an end to this business arrangement, at all costs. She knew enough about the law to know that a spouse could not be compelled to testify against the other partner. Jurisprudence was her benefactor in going forward with her plan. Some cases with less structure had tilted from time to time, but not here—she was sure of that.

Now, she thought. *Which one will I marry? Perhaps Cleadeth. He has some brains and a bit of social decorum . . . Well, that may be stretching it, but at least he's not Elmer.*

TWO WEEKS LATER THE WEDDING WAS ALL SET. THEY'D decided to save money and stand before the justice of the peace. Clea wore his black suit without the black tie and was so nervous he had to pee every ten minutes.

Elmer stood on the sidelines making an astute observation along with a prediction: *This wedding will never take place!* This was a scene hard to imagine, ole Clea standing next to Mrs. Dixon. The black material of Clea's pant legs was just a-quivering.

No sooner had that thought cleared his mind than three sheriff's deputies came through the front door. Two headed straight for Mrs. Dixon, seizing her by the elbow, while the other one stood with his hand resting on the butt of his holstered gun.

As Clea stood watching his life being saved, he thought it was like some good Joe coming along and cutting him down from the gallows, and right at that moment the sun came out brighter than he had ever seen in is life. *Yes, I will live to tell the story*. It was like a spiritual moment. A blessing right before his eyes. Clea stayed his distance so as not to interfere with Fate doing what Fate does best—that is, to correct wrongs.

When things were settling down, Elmer raised his eyes to the heavens and uttered quietly, "Thank you, God."

One of the deputies thanked the boys for the tip about

the murder. As the other two walked the arrested bride out, they paused and Mrs. Dixon whispered to Clea, "You just lost access to three million dollars, you fool."

The news of three million dollars was more than Clea could bear: his tricky bladder was starting to worry him. He quickly dashed outside for a tree.

✦

THE TWINS

Victoria Glaze sat shaking and sobbing and crying over the death of her husband, Ott Glaze.

Her sister, Ollie Ray, scolded her. "For Pete's sake, quit ballin' your eyes out. He was a no-account anyway."

Victoria shot back, "How dare you say such a thing about my dead husband! He was a good man."

Ollie, who was seated on the ottoman in the parlor, rose to her feet as her sister stood before her.

In one fluid motion, Victoria pulled a small, tarnished derringer from her cotton handbag and shot Ollie in the heart. Dead!

The sheriff confirmed this woman was mean.

The parishioners applauded with gusto. The pastor stepped out into the aisle between the pews and thanked the twins for a magnificent performance. The pastor reminded them that when this play was over the programs committee would be working on the Christmas play—a more palatable story, filled with love and grace and miracles.

The twins lived in a large Victorian home up on Rose Hill Road, where they had lived for the last fifty years or so. Victoria really did have a husband who'd died, and his name really was Ott. Ollie, on the other hand, had never married, but she did have gentlemen suitors, who these days were usually retired business leaders.

That night after the twins' rousing performance, large snowflakes blanketed the ground with a record snowfall, and the next morning Ollie went out in the horse-drawn sleigh. It was pulled by old Newt, who had been a family member these eighteen years past. His age caused him to be skittish at times, but this morning he was calm and dedicated to his task. The sleigh hadn't even gotten past the house when suddenly the weight of the new snow caused a tree limb to break. It crashed to the ground next to Newt, who suddenly found new energy, rearing up and whinnying like he was trapped in a burning barn.

Victoria heard the commotion and moved into the living room so she could watch the fun through the large bay windows. She wished it were she who was having fun, but that quickly changed when she saw Ollie was in trouble.

Without her coat, Victoria dashed out into the street to help Ollie. She was reaching for the bit and bridle, but ole Newt threw his head up and back, which caused Victoria to lose her balance in the snow. Newt, still not under control, heaved forward and stepped on Victoria's legs, though breaking just the one.

Finally, a neighbor arrived and was able to subdue Newt. Without any further incident, the neighbor lifted Victoria onto the seat of the sleigh and headed Newt in the direction of the hospital.

Ollie, over the years, had gained some insight as to when and when not to enter the social circle when it concerned Victoria. She watched from the sidelines, where family members were relegated when Victoria was at work.

The good neighbor's name was Oliver, and Victoria wasn't about to let an opportunity go to waste. She had learned to do her sobbing for any reason, and this was a good reason—pity.

At the hospital, Victoria did just what was necessary to expedite her discharge from those silly young nurses, and she and Oliver were out of there in nothing flat. On the way home, a slight dusting of snow began to fall at the right time. Victoria snuggled up against Oliver, in search of additional warmth, she claimed. She slipped her arm through his and managed to lay her head on his shoulder, inquiring if that made controlling ole Newt any harder. Not at all, Oliver was quick to reply.

She pointed out they were coming up on the cutoff to Birdie County, where it was easy to get a license and married all in the same evening. She didn't even have to bat her phony eyelashes. She heard the command "Whoa on, old Newt" and felt the sleigh leaning to the left as he made the turn.

Within thirty minutes, her last name was changed—married! The new couple got a jug of moonshine to celebrate, and in the cold weather, the nips went on and on until the jug was empty and tossed to the side, only a pause in the celebration.

Gone for hours, the two burst into the house loud and excited. The inebriated seventy-nine-year-old sister had lost it this time. She started in with, "We're married!" The same line went on and on until she took the time to introduce her husband, Oliver.

Ollie was horrified by the behavior and conduct of these two. They were out-of-their-minds drunk on liquor and blinded to reality. *Victoria, who holds herself out to be so smart, has done it this time,* Ollie thought. *She forgot Daddy's will clearly states if one of the sisters should marry, then and there she immediately forfeits her part of the inheritance. Oh boy, this will be fun.*

"I suppose you two will be running off for a little quickie honeymoon, right?"

They nodded.

While Victoria was upstairs packing, Ollie dove into a stirring conversation with Oliver to gain more knowledge about lover boy. "Oliver, what is your line of employment?"

After a period of finding composure and what seemed like building up courage, he said, "Well, I've been out of work for some time now."

Ollie said, "Oh boy, is that right?"

"Yes."

"Have you been married before?"

"Twice," Oliver replied. "But that's not correct. I've been married twice and eloped another time, but she ran out and I haven't seen her since. Please forgive my stuttering; I get in a hurry and that's what happens."

"Really . . ." was all Ollie could get out before she started sniffling and dabbing her nose with her hankie.

Victoria swung around the newel post and declared, "I'm here! Let's go, Oliver Dolliver!"

The newlyweds joyfully headed to the front door; off to where, Ollie had no clue. Ollie said goodbye as she raced out of the room crying.

DAYS LATER A STARTLING AND UNEXPECTED EVENT TOOK place as the lovebirds returned from nuptial bliss. Victoria and Oliver Dolliver entered the parlor, where Ollie sat flipping through, not really reading, *The Saturday Evening Post.* They stood before her grinning like Cheshire Cats.

Victoria was the first to speak. "Ollie, that was my best performance ever! Oliver is an actor over in Duncan County, and we thought we would put on a show for you. You see, Ollie, we really aren't married."

"Well, according to this marriage license you sure are. Period."

"Oh, that's just an old silly piece of paper."

"Did you copulate?"

"Ollie, I do that all the time. That doesn't ring any bells."

"No, I suppose it doesn't—not with you anyway," Ollie said in a state of exasperation. "Let me tell you what you have gone and done, Miss Victoria. You have seriously usurped our wonderful daddy's will."

"What do you mean?" Victoria's voice and words carried concern.

"If you marry, your part of the will is automatically and immediately null and void. Sister, you and this charlatan have robbed yourselves of your comfortable lifestyle."

It was then that Oliver interceded and with concern and surprise said, "You mean I have—or I mean to say *we* have—no money?"

"The way you started to say it and then finally said it are the same—NO!" said Ollie.

Oliver looked woebegone.

"Why, Oliver, if I didn't know better, I would say that you thought you were picking low-hanging fruit, didn't you?"

Ollie, while Oliver was still present, told Victoria, "The attorney said if you get an annulment immediately, he will petition the court to reinstate you into the will—if I am in agreement."

Color returned to Victoria's face, but she anxiously waited to hear Ollie say she would agree to the conditions. She walked slowly towards her, practically sitting on Ollie's lap they were so close.

"Victoria, you have always been so impatient." Ollie saw Victoria was becoming angrier by the minute.

Victoria finally burst out, "Ollie, you are now, and you have always been, a selfish bitch!"

Ollie remained calm, and Victoria stomped out of the room using curse words so strong that Ollie didn't even know some of them.

When Victoria came back into the room, she looked like she had finished a nasty fight and lost. Along with her physical presence was a mind full of hateful words. With each word spewed at Ollie, her anger intensified—to the point that she threw a vase at Ollie.

When Victoria saw that was not achieving the desired effect, she pulled the notorious tarnished derringer from her cotton bag and handed it over to Ollie. "Here, I don't want to see that gun again. Ollie, I swear I'm likely to kill myself over what I've done to poor daddy."

Ollie got up, walked over to the lace curtains, and pulled one back carefully to be sure that old Oliver dildo or whatever his name was had in fact left. Satisfied with what she saw, or *didn't* see in this case, Ollie said, "Victoria, when will you go down and get the annulment?"

Victoria didn't like Ollie watching her squirm.

"Well, what's your answer?"

Victoria said, "Not so fast—I'm still on my honeymoon."

"What?!" Ollie could barely speak. "Now listen, you over-the-hill, old, worn-out, varicose prostitute. I may be your sister, but I'm not going to be your caretaker. You go down to that lawyer tomorrow first thing, or I swear I'll have you thrown out of this house! And I better not see that loser back here!"

Victoria shot back, "I will get it annulled first thing in the morning, but please don't call me those awful names."

Ollie looked at Victoria. "Honey, come over here and sit next to me and I'll let you in on some good news."

Victoria sat on the sofa next to Ollie, and with her head down, pouting, said, "What's the good news?"

"Here's the good news: I was just making up the story

about Daddy's will and meeting with an attorney. Your position hasn't changed one little bit. I just don't think that Oliver character is good for you—all he wants is your money."

Victoria jumped up and started pacing. She twisted her hankie around her fingers. Finally, she said, "You tricked us? Mean. That's all. That is just plain old meanness. Ollie, I'm your sister! Why did you do that?"

"I wanted to save you from that money-grabbing widow's-peak scavenger, that's why," Ollie said.

"Why, we never did consummate our marriage that night. The first night of our honeymoon, there I sat next to this wonderful man who was filled with passion and raring to go. We were lounging on the chaise, and the wine was flowing. He was as still as a mouse and then he reached over, loosened the drawstring on my pajama top, and started snoring—asleep! Need I say the honeymoon was over—and I do mean over."

Ollie gleefully asked, "Victoria, you mean you're still a 'virgin'?"

"Yes," Victoria said, batting her fake eyelashes. "Thanks to my drawstrings."

✦

THE AERIALIST

RHONDA WAS TENSE, NOT ABOUT DOING HER aerial act, but about her personal life. *I sure hope Mr. Crawley can't see the worried look on my face way up here*, she thought. Up high on the pedestal and flying through the air above the crowd she was at ease, she was a star, she was a skilled flying trapeze artist. Wherever the circus performed, crowds came to see her doing what she did best. But down on the ground, it was a different life; the one who claimed to love her didn't know the meaning of the word.

From high up, she could watch the crowd scramble for the best seat and the rambunctious kids running around taunting other kids, mostly smaller ones. Watching the kids made her smile. *Simpler times*, she thought. She wore a white costume adorned with rhinestones and sequins that glittered with her every move. Curious little girls would come up to her and gently run their little hands over the "glittery things" as they called them, and then they would run off to find Mom and Dad. The gleeful children brought a big smile to her face.

However, the slightest glimpse of Renaldo was too much. Her heart filled with sadness; the pain of rejection was heavy. His job fit him perfectly, for he was responsible for cleaning out the cages—and now it was time to clean him out.

In the circus life, it was common to meet and fall in love easily, but marriage was not too certain. Brief relationships would come and go. There was little chance to meet others outside the big tent. It was also common to have more than one serious lover; in Renaldo's case, he had Beth, and for some reason thought Rhonda wouldn't hear about her. Rhonda had never met or seen Beth; in fact, she never really cared one way or the other about her. She liked being in control of her emotions and not letting her mind rule her too much.

Lately, Bobby had been on her mind with greater frequency. Bobby was a kind and gentle person, who in this case was also a real lifesaver. Every time she let go of the trapeze bar and leaped in his direction, she knew he would be there. Then, she had a thought that brought on a chill and a shiver: if Renaldo were the one there to catch her, would she feel as safe and secure? It took her a few minutes to find a truthful answer to that question. She gazed up looking for Bobby but saw nothing. Smitten for Bobby? Well, maybe a little bit. Suddenly she pursed her mouth and her forehead followed suit. *Renaldo was a mean person.* There she finally said it outright, and it felt good to her to be honest with herself.

RHONDA WAS ADMIRED FOR HER WELL-COORDINATED moves on the bars and for her sweet personality. All of the other performers liked her. Jealousy didn't infect every performer but popped up from time to time and was always in play with some who seemed to thrive on it. Performers were cautious because sabotage could be a part of jealousy. One evening when Rhonda returned to her dressing room to get ready for the next show, she found her costume ripped into pieces. That same evening, Bobby's rigging was tampered with, which took hours to correct. Jealousy knows no boundaries when you work in such small confines and have limited freedom in the outside world, but overall, it was not common behavior.

Moreover, the circus people tended to be united as a family. Ed Crawley, or "Mr. Ed Crawley" as the employees called him, was the owner of Big Tent Enterprise. All the employees respected him immensely because he treated them fairly and looked out for their interest. He paid close attention to the well-being of the females; the men thought they were Romeos under the tent, and the young women were too inexperienced to handle the suave, muscle-bound hero type, especially the ones who had not yet developed the quick "put you in your place and not bruise your ego too much" to keep their distance. Mr. Crawley was very much aware of their starry-eyed perception of these men who had a tattoo and a line for every young "chick."

The crowd eagerly waited for the show to begin. The air was filled with all the smells one would expect at a circus: fresh popcorn, cotton candy, hotdogs, a hodgepodge of animals, and a slight scent of old canvas warming in the hot summer sun. The excitement increased with each passing minute; impatience was always present with big crowds and the dazzling performance of Rhonda Farr.

Rhonda descended to the base of the pole to wait for her introduction and cue. Her costume glittered in the lights. She knew Mr. Crawley was in the shadows somewhere for this part of the opening. *He never misses it,* thought Rhonda. Then the lights in the big top darkened and the mood intensified. The drummer did a couple of downbeats and ended with drum rolls precisely when the spotlight illuminated the ringmaster. He was dressed in a black tuxedo with tails and a top hat, and he carried a black cane that he used for emphasis. From that pinpoint of light in the darkness of the big top came his cry for the show to begin.

"Ladies and gentlemen and children of all ages! Welcome to the Crawley Brothers' Circus under the big top." He paused. "They fly through the air with the greatest of ease. As ever, the beauty, grace, and daring of the flying trapeze!" He paused again for effect. "Presenting now . . . the Flying Skyes!"

The spotlight moved to the troupe standing at the base of the pole. Rhonda, Bobby, Connie, and Thomas delighted in taking their deserved bows. The crowd roared with joy and hollered just to share their excitement. Rhonda's heart was racing, and the adrenalin was flowing, and she felt an amazing amount of calm and strength through all the excitement. With a sense of security, she thought, *This is my life. I love the exhilaration. Not even when I was a child and put on plays for my family and neighbors did I experience anything close to this.* She knew this was the moment. She thought the buildup would never end, but end it did and she was ready to perform.

"And now, in the center ring, we have the daring and brave aerialist, Rhonda Farr . . ." The ringmaster had to pause because the noise was so loud, he was being drowned out. ". . . who will perform her death-defying acrobatic stunts in midair. Now, ladies and gentlemen, a little sidebar about Rhonda: she started performing before she could drive a car. And now look at her: she flies where cars can't go, close to the stars!"

The spotlight focused on Rhonda as she ascended the ladder; her bottom swung from side to side putting on a sparkling light show as the spot reflected off her glittery costume. She continued with this well-rehearsed performance to the pedestal where the rest of the troupe had already taken their places.

On the pedestal she rehearsed the act in her mind. She held the bar with her right hand and steadied herself with her left as she stood next to the mast and visualized the rhythm and timing. Connie joined her so she could hook the bar once Rhonda left it in mid-flight. Rhonda looked across at Bobby; he was the grabber, meaning he was the one who would catch Rhonda when she leaped to the next bar. This was a dream come true for Bobby. He was in charge of and called the direction for the troupe. Thomas was there also, as backup. Rhonda's and Bobby's eyes met. It was necessary to connect eye to eye with the people you worked with, especially if your life depended on them. Rhonda made sure that Bobby saw her eyes communicate, "I'm counting on you to save my life." Rhonda knew the grabber called the shots; he was the one who timed the flights—it was all up to him. Bobby was standing on his pedestal ready to swing out, but right before he did, he shouted, "Hut!" When Rhonda and Connie heard the command, they went into action.

Rhonda swung off. She would swing towards the grabber, and on the second swing she would leap and perform a somersault in midair where the grabber would catch her. In the meantime, Connie would have successfully hooked the swing left vacant by Rhonda. Rhonda was confident that Bobby would be there to grab her wrists. He was, and the crowd rewarded them with loud applause.

Rhonda and Bobby were swinging back to the original starting pedestal. Connie was ready to release the vacant swing when Bobby shouted the command—the success of the stunt depended on her sending the bar at the right time. Bobby shouted, "Hut," and Connie pushed the swing into the path that both Bobby and Rhonda were on in midair.

Rhonda was ready when Bobby let go, but in this instance, he gave a little flip so she could do a perfect midair somersault, grab the bar as she was falling, and swing up and land on the pedestal where it all began. With a big smile on her face, Rhonda took two small bows. The crowd loved every move that she made.

Rhonda remembered a show about two years earlier when the same troupe had been performing and she'd insisted on doing a double somersault and a twist all in the same flight. She clearly remembered, when the time came, seeing the tension on Bobby's face and the worry in his eyes. It was a look she had never seen before and hadn't seen since. Rhonda figured they'd rehearsed the stunt close to two dozen times with no incidents, which was pretty good in this business. The thing that had caused the crowd to come to their feet as the stunt took place was that she had been blindfolded.

They'd decided that an edge of safety was needed, so she had been without a blindfold while preparing and waiting for the command from Bobby. Just before Bobby called out "Hut," the blindfold had been quickly slipped over her eyes. All she remembered was "Hut" and the lump in her throat as she jumped off in faith swinging to Bobby somewhere out there unseen. She loved the risk and the rush and the blood pumping!

When Bobby had known it was the right speed, all that had remained was luck. He'd hollered, "Hut," and Rhonda had leaped in what she thought was the right direction and grabbed onto warm flesh. Right away Bobby had noticed how sweaty her hands were—and his too. Then had come the really risky part: the return to the original pedestal. This time no one would be there to catch Rhonda; she was on her own. So much was at stake. Connie needed to swing the bar so it would arrive at the exact time Rhonda leaped for it. Bobby would shout the command "Hut" and there would be a very small window for her to jump and catch the bar before falling to the net. Anytime a performer fell to the net, it was interpreted as "hitting the ground" because it was considered a mistake.

Bobby had a firm grip on her, and he started to pump with his body to get some speed up. Being upside down and holding onto Rhonda, he needed to be extra careful in calculating the timing of it all. He said to Rhonda as they swung back and forth, "We are getting close to leap time. Okay, this is the last swing up. The next time I'll call the command and give you the little flip. As you start falling to the ground reach out and grab the bar. Give a strong pump and expect to land on the pedestal. Connie will be there to grab you and get you on the pedestal, but don't panic and pull her off." Bobby knew those repetitive reminders were necessary to keep her focused. Moreover, Rhonda was still facing backwards from the leap. When she let go from Bobby and was traveling to Connie, she would spin around, making it easier for Connie to assist her onto the platform.

"Get ready," Bobby said. "Here it is . . . Hut!"

And then she'd been in the air.

She remembered how exciting the blindfolded stunt had been to perform—and how furious Mr. Crawley had been that he hadn't been informed of it in advance.

Tonight's crowd was going crazy; people were applauding

loudly and stomping their feet. There were whispers about how smoothly and confidently Rhonda had performed.

She was done for the night. Next came the other entertainers and then the animals, including the lion tamer. The clowns amused people of all ages. When all the events were over and as the big top emptied out, people were still talking about Rhonda. Where would she be performing next?

Rhonda was going to see Bobby tonight for some big-tent "cuisine," which meant hot dogs with chili and Coca-Colas and some old stale popcorn. They laughed at this less-than-fine example of fine dining.

They were in the middle of having a good time when Renaldo showed up, strutting around acting and sounding tough. Bobby had his fill and stood up. He blocked Renaldo's path with a look of "I dare you" on his face. When Renaldo walked past Bobby, he deliberately bumped his shoulder, almost causing him to lose his balance, but Bobby didn't take the bait.

As the days and weeks passed, Rhonda and Bobby were seen together more and more, often times laughing with gentle fooling around. "Two people in love" would be the right description. It was well established that they were a couple; it was equally well established that Renaldo was as angry as a Brahma bull. It was also noted that Mr. Crawley warned Renaldo there had better not be any trouble.

BOBBY MET RHONDA OUTSIDE HER DRESSING ROOM AND informed her that he was adding a new member to the team. Rhonda liked the idea of having another member who could relieve the demands on everyone else. Bobby informed her that Bethany had some experience and had trained with a smaller outfit on the high wire. "You will be directly in charge of her."

Rhonda raised her eyebrows when she heard the name Bethany; she knew her as Beth. But she wasn't going to let the fact that it was Renaldo's new girlfriend bother her. She said to Bobby, "I'm a team player!" But as he walked away, she thought, *Who is this Bethany, really? It irks me some, but as I said, I'm a team player.*

The next morning Rhonda was eager to meet her new protégé and begin the hard work of developing a star aerialist. They introduced themselves briefly; after hearing about Bethany's experiences, she sent her up the ladder to take a swing. Bethany swung out and leaped to the next bar, which was passed off by Thomas.

When Bethany came down, Rhonda immediately criticized her performance, which she evaluated as having bad timing. "That timing was so poor that someone is going to fall to the net."

After a couple more hours of Rhonda watching and criticizing her, Bethany said, "Let's call it a day and start over in the morning." As she walked away, she added, "And perhaps you could consider a more diplomatic approach."

Rhonda stopped and looked at her. "Bethany, I think you have an abundance of talent, but we need to bring it in line with the rest of the troupe. Timing is important in the routines that we perform." *Team player*, she reminded herself. *I'm a team player.*

RHONDA AND BOBBY WERE ON THEIR WAY TO SOME MORE "fine dining." The show that afternoon had been especially good, and they were bubbling about the audience's reaction.

They got their chili dogs and Cokes and sat at one of the outdoor tables. A few tables over sat Renaldo and Bethany. Renaldo was leaning in towards her, talking furiously with an intense look on his face.

Rhonda said, "You know if Renaldo sees us together, he'll be jealous. And angry."

"I don't care," Bobby shot back.

Rhonda and Bobby tried to ignore the other couple, but Renaldo's voice kept getting louder, and Bethany seemed to keep shrinking at his words.

"You stupid idiot! You're such a loser!"

Bobby got up. "Hey, man. Leave her alone. There's no need to talk to anyone like that."

"Keep your nose out of it, Bobby-boy. This is none of your business."

"Renaldo, knock it off or I'll call Mr. Crawley. You're skating on thin ice."

Renaldo shoved Bobby to the ground. While Bobby lay there, Renaldo straddled him and taunted him to get up and fight. "Coward!"

Bobby, using his shoulders and the heels of both feet, raised up and swung his backside to the left; using his right foot, he caught Renaldo in the back of his knees, causing him to buckle to the ground.

With Renaldo off him, Bobby was up in an instant. As Renaldo tried to get up, his rear was in a perfect position for

Bobby to give him a swift kick to the seat of his pants, which he did beautifully. Some of the other performers clapped their hands in approval.

As Bobby walked away brushing the dust off his pants, Renaldo shouted, "I'll get even with you for that."

Rhonda walked up beside Beth and said quietly, "I understand how difficult Renaldo can be. If you ever need a friend to talk to, that's me." Then she ran to catch up with Bobby.

DURING THE NEXT SHOW, WHICH WAS PACKED, PEOPLE were standing in places that were against the fire marshal's approval. But the ushers hurriedly brought them folding chairs, so they could comfortably enjoy the show.

Bobby and Rhonda stood on the pedestal together waiting for their part. Rhonda whispered out of the corner of her mouth, "I don't feel right about things. I'm uneasy. Something just doesn't feel right. Renaldo has been acting very weird around me. He just glares at me in a mean sort of way."

"Yes, me too," Bobby replied.

"Get ready—we're up next," Rhonda said.

Bobby swung off, but Rhonda saw the puzzled look on his face as he glanced back at her. She knew she was supposed to be swinging out by this point, but she felt frozen in place.

Bobby turned so he was facing Rhonda again and swung up on the pedestal. The look in his eyes showed concern.

"Let's go," he said.

Bobby again swung out and looked back at her. She still didn't move. She saw Beth on the opposite pedestal shaking her head.

Rhonda was becoming frustrated. She said to herself, *The heck with it—I'm going.*

She swung out, and Bobby swung towards her, and on the next swing, he said, "Jump!" As he reached the apex on the backswing, he called out, "Hut!"

They were swinging towards each other. Bobby was holding on with his feet twisted and hooked on the side ropes. It was time, and she didn't follow the command, she didn't jump.

Bobby got himself seated upright on the swing and stared at her. He built up speed and landed on the pedestal next to her.

She was breathless and afraid.

"Hey, what's going on with you?"

"Something is going to happen. I just know it."

"No, you don't know it. You are imagining it. Renaldo has you petrified."

"All right, all right, I'm ready. Let's go. I'll be fine. Swing off."

Bobby swung off and slid to his knees with his feet hooked on the side ropes. Then he swung back to meet her.

Rhonda swung off and was about to climb in speed when suddenly one of her ropes snapped. As she fell to the net, she looked up and saw a look on Beth's face that screamed *No*.

In the net, Rhonda remained lifeless. The big tent crowd was silent and motionless. Had she passed out from the shock of the fall? Or had she broken her neck?

As Rhonda stirred, the crowd quickly stood up. She made her way to the edge of the net to somersault off, but she knew that Bobby was coming to be with her, so she waited for him, and together they rolled out of the net.

The crowd went crazy.

AFTER THE SHOW, BOBBY WALKED RHONDA BACK TO her tent. They walked silently, having exhausted all speculation about whether Rhonda's fall was a freak accident or sabotage by Renaldo.

As they passed by Beth's, they couldn't help but hear someone sobbing and a loud voice talking in a cruel manner.

As Bobby and Rhonda got closer to the tent, there was no mistake that Bethany and Renaldo were having a loud argument and that Bethany was crying.

Rhonda glanced at Bobby. "We have to help."

As Bobby was about to knock on the door, they heard the sound of a smack on flesh. Bobby didn't bother to knock. He barged in and saw Renaldo smack Bethany hard in the face again. He then grabbed Renaldo's arm before he could deliver another blow and spun him around. He was ready to slug him in the kisser but at the last second decided against it.

He took some time to study Renaldo's face, and then with a stern expression and an angry voice told him that if he ever set foot on the grounds again, he would beat the shit out of him. As Renaldo was about to walk away Bobby said, "I intend to mess you up really bad, so heed my warning: don't come back!"

Much to everyone's surprise, Renaldo walked off, slowly and with his head down. His stride projected it was all over; he was defeated.

Beth told Rhonda and Bobby that she had severed all ties with Renaldo and that's why he had blown up. She had gotten fed up with the things that would spill from his mouth during his fits of anger—how much he despised Bobby and hated the sight of him. "I've never heard such dislike for another living soul. And he was the one who cut your rope tonight."

"I figured," said Rhonda.

The three took turns hugging each other.

Beth said jokingly, "I'd better get an invitation to the big day!"

Once Beth was settled, Bobby and Rhonda continued to Rhonda's tent, his arm comfortably around her waist. Out of nowhere, the silence was broken when a shot rang out, shattering the moment of bliss for two lovers. Rhonda screamed. Bobby lay on the ground bleeding from a shoulder wound. Renaldo stood frozen there, arms at his side, a gun held loosely in one. Those who had gathered out of concern and curiosity stood quietly. In the distance, the sound of a police siren wailed.

✦

FLYING THE COOP

MY NAME IS CARTER-WRAY HONEYCUTT. I'M editor-in-chief for the *Sunny Times* daily news. In one of my first editorial columns, I wrote, "Isn't it funny how one person can toil their entire life, sunup to sundown, and do poorly, while someone else of comparable standing does next to nothing and fares better? How can that be?"

I think some answers might exist in the story of Clarence Bieterman, who represents the first person, the one who toils and misses out on life because he works all the time. Then there is old Ernie Plowman, who sleeps until noon every day and barely manages to milk two cows and feed a dozen scrawny chickens. His wife flew the coop long ago. The only puzzling question is why the chickens haven't done what Mrs. Plowman up and did.

One day Ernie was in the hardware store talking to Matt Garrison, the proprietor. Ernie was talking big stuff and trying to be Mr. Hot Shot, as he often did.

Matt spoke up. "Plowman, since you are the town's bank on two legs, why don't you invest in one of these new lottery tickets?" As he said this to Ernie, Matt leaned on the counter, his forearms exposed. Matt liked to show off his muscular arms, plus the new Timex watch he was wearing now that he sold them. "Look," he said. "It's simple. You lay down twenty dollars, and if your numbers are drawn, you stand a chance to win fifty thousand dollars. Now I know that's chicken feed to you." (These are words that Matt shared with me almost verbatim.)

The word "chicken" turned Ernie's stomach. He was forced to think of his paltry critters. He was ashamed that he couldn't raise healthy, plump chickens. (When you know Ernie, you can just read his face and know exactly what he's thinking.)

Clarence Bieterman, however, had no time for idle gossip, nor for gambling his money on a lottery ticket. Instead, he was busy on his farm clearing off the bottom section of old sagebrush and some rotten thistle weed. The old hedge apple tree needed to come down, but it had gotten so big now it would take two good men to do it. He stood for the longest time just staring at the tree from base to the top and after some uninterrupted time at this he said, "Yep, going to need some help." He wanted to expand his planting land to increase his income per bushel, but he was growing tired most of the time and found his ambition had dwindled considerably. (But I've visited his place on two occasions and Clarence runs a clean and tidy farm.)

One day after the conversation with Ernie, Matt received a letter from a brokerage house pertaining to the lottery that Mr. Plowman had invested in, along with a certified check for fifty thousand dollars and no cents. Matt caught the last part of the written section of the check where it said "no cents." He tried to hold back a chuckle, but he let it go just as Ernie walked through the front door.

"What's so funny?" asked Ernie.

Matt replied with a mysterious answer in the form of a question. "Do you have your pickup truck here today?"

Ernie remained puzzled. "Why?"

Matt slid the check and letter to him to study. "You may need it to get all this money home."

Ernie just stood for the longest time without moving or saying a word. He stared at the letter and then at the check, and back and forth he went, on and on, until Matt pointed out that his pickup was still idling in front of the store.

Matt made a good business decision by not mentioning a word of this to any of his customers and never entering into a discussion if someone brought it up. Matt did hear that Ernie gave half the winnings to his church and put the other half in the bank.

CLARENCE BIETERMAN OWNED A SMALL BUT WELL-maintained house near a riverbed that had been dry for so long it was referred to as "the dry bed," but at some point there must have been water running through it because there was evidence of serious fishing at one time or another. Rusty hooks were found where they had snagged on the edge of a big rough rock and the line broke as the fisherman had tugged to free the line. When asked, Clarence would defend his property and the wisdom that went into purchasing the ill-fated location. Years before he shucked out the money, he had heard that the state was going to create a dam on a much larger river, and when that happened the water would be forced to once again flow right down past his front porch where he could sit and fish without getting out of his rocking chair.

Sure enough, in several months the state did what they'd said they would and in no time, there sat old Clarence casting a baited hook from his cushioned rocking chair. In thinking back, he said he remembered hearing a lot of blasting but never gave it any thought. But as a result, he had fresh fish twice a day every day and enjoyed the many different methods of cooking his catch. But good manners prevailed, and Clarence would never burp at the end of a scrumptious meal; he concluded that was gloating. His shirt sleeves were spotless—no food stains. The older women in town admired his manners and personal neatness.

A RUMOR WAS CIRCULATING ABOUT ERNIE, WHO HAD become jealous over Clarence's good fortune with the river. Along with jealously came revenge—sometimes nothing more than a tinge of revenge as the saying goes. The question on everyone's mind was, in what form would Ernie take revenge? Some of the townspeople said, "Well there you are—the tenth commandment says 'Thou shalt not covet.'" It's not limited to a wife; it's about what your neighbor has and you wanting one too. Poor Ernie.

The beginning of this story laid out for study why this person or that person outdid the other. Well, it's simple: in life, good things and bad things come to each of us at different intervals and in different ways.

Look at it in pieces: Ernie's success was well-known around town—or was it?

Ernie might brag and act really big, but to my knowledge, not one single person can testify to his financial success. Not a single balance sheet has ever been seen. Besides, a person's riches are not measured by their bank balance; real success is best measured by their character and how they treat people. Lastly, what counts in life is the ability to forgive and forget, followed by an apology if necessary. It may seem silly, but it's even tallied up by how you treat your animals, especially your dog. (Notice I never mentioned a cat.)

You never heard one word from Clarence when Ernie won fifty thousand dollars, not one. He was busy tilling his soil to increase the land's value. I'm not a runner, but if I were, I'd say never look back to see how close the closest person is because it distracts from your concentration on the job at hand.

But back to Ernie and his jealousy . . . Matt Garrison became very concerned—so concerned that he called me in a hysterical frame of mind, telling me about Ernie driving off with dynamite bouncing around in the back of his truck.

He said Ernie came pulling up in front of the hardware store and dashed in kind of crazy acting, raising his voice at Matt telling him he needed a case of dynamite.

Matt told him, "Ernie, that's a lot of bang. What in heaven's name are you fixing to do?"

Apparently, Ernie had no time to talk and said his truck was running, drinking up gas. Ernie just dropped the dynamite and the blasting caps in the bed of the truck and off he flew down the road.

Matt took the time to notice a couple of unusual things about Ernie. First, he had a tie on, which was tied around his bare neck, because he was wearing no shirt, just long johns. Secondly, he had shaved, which was a rare occurrence.

I remained at my desk deep in thought about what Matt had just told me. Then I jumped up from my chair in shock at a boom so powerful and loud that my ears were ringing. The other folks in the office looked around as if wherever their eyes landed there would be the answer.

Then I wondered what the boom was all about, and the empty spot in my mind was filled with the only logical answer: Ernie.

As I drove by the hardware store, Matt was putting the Closed sign on the locked door. As he ran to cross the street, I gave a big horn honk and stopped, and he jumped in my car. We raced out to Ernie's farm.

"The only explanation is that the dynamite got jostled too much and ignited," Matt proclaimed.

Each hill we crested was filled with the tension of what we might find, and after one particularly big, bumpy hill, I slammed on the breaks because of what I saw. Metal, tires—some still on the rims—and pieces of rubber everywhere. There were parts of the motor, and Matt was sure one of the heads from the motor was blown off and lying in the middle of the road. Poor Ernie. Poor, poor Ernie.

We looked and looked, and we were sure there were chicken feathers and chicken parts covering the highway too.

"I'll be damned! This is a sight to see."

I looked over at Matt and surprise was revealed by his expression. Without thinking, I said, "Those chickens finally did fly the coop." And at last, I asked, "This is the elephant in the room question: do you see anything that resembles Ernie?"

Quietness settled over us and seemed like it might stay.

Matt finally broke the spell. "Well, the chicken parts make it hard, unless old Ernie had feathers for a beard, but today he was clean-shaven when he came in the store."

As we continued to wander around in the road looking for signs of Ernie, up rolled Clarence going so slow the car looked like it was coasting. As he sauntered up, he asked in a loud voice, "What you all just walking around fer?"

When he was told about Ernie, he started laughing so hard he started coughing. Finally he was able to catch his breath, but not without spitting the mucus from his lungs.

"Clarence," I said, "you might want to see Doc Barber about that cough."

"Maybe so," he said.

Every time Clarence was warming up to say something, he would lick his lips. "Listen, you two. I need to let you in on a little news before you walk yourselves crazy. Ole Ernie is over at my place."

Our mouths dropped open, and simultaneously Matt and I replied, "What?"

Clarence said, "Listen, I know Ernie can be difficult at times—and honestly, can't we all? I went last week to see him, and I invited him to come on over to my place for some beers and to enjoy the use of my rocking chair and catch all the fish he wanted."

"What about the explosion? The truck? And all these dead chickens?"

"He stopped to let the chickens run free so they could do better in the wild than at his place. He had carried all the crates of chickens except for one down to the bank of the river, and as he was walking back up the bank, he heard the explosion. So he turned around and went back to the river and followed it to my front porch and there I sat."

Life sure can be a mystery. One day you think you've got everything all figured out and put together, and then things like this happen. Then you are back to square one and realize you haven't given human beings enough credit for working out their own puzzle pieces.

✦

NORMA'S LAST SPLASH

It was the beginning of June and doors and windows were wide open. The fragrance of magnolia blossoms swished through the house filling every room, and then the next minute the wonderfulness was gone and in its place was the smell of biscuits and fried chicken. A new wonderfulness.

Mr. Edgar Potsworth was pleased when he got the call to come down for Sunday brunch because he too smelled his favorites, biscuits and fried chicken. But he also smelled something else that he didn't care too much about. Edgar's olfactory nerve was super keen that day and he was willing to judge his sniffing as conclusive, final, and incontrovertible. The farther he descended the flight of stairs, the closer he got to remembering the name of the woman who had a horrible habit of splashing a whole bottle of Swish Alps Snowfall Refreshing Summer Splash all over her body. The name Swish was a bad play on words, meaning the splash would swish away staleness and invigorate the body to a new high.

Two steps from the bottom of the staircase, it hit him who the mystery woman was. Before he even whispered the two-syllable name to himself he felt a little queasy at his stomach.

Edgar was in his third year at Miss Peggy Fielders's boardinghouse; he had become one of the family, even to the point that Miss Fielders would scold him severely for not putting his dress shoes in the closet in his own room. As Edgar entered the dining room, he did a quick visual sweep of those at the table. Just like a man of good breeding, he came to stand at the back of his chair with his hand resting gently on the yoke. He slowly spoke to each seated person in turn, looking them in the eye and wishing them a good day before seating himself.

Mr. Chubb Berry was the custodian at the local school and considered himself important simply because he was a ten-year veteran at the boardinghouse. He would deliberately taunt Miss Fielders to the point that she became exasperated with him, and then it would spill over to everyone else.

Seated next to Mr. Berry was Mr. William Barely, who was a representative for the Buster Brown Shoe Company and barely said a word. And seated next to Mr. Barely was Miss Lillian Crabtree, who was referred to as Lilly because she said it made her feel younger.

Next to Lilly was Mrs. Cromer, who regularly entertained everyone with her poetry readings; sometimes she read a poem she'd written herself, but mostly it was Longfellow she quoted. She would become very emotional when she read Longfellow's poem "I Heard the Bells on Christmas Day." It was always halfway through that she would pause and tell the story about his wife who had died of an accidental fire and then, as if it were needed, she would tell the grueling story of their son being seriously injured in battle. The women would be in tears or at least sniffling into their dainty hankies with delicate embroidery work on the edges; the men would become quiet and thoughtful. Her performances were momentarily entertaining, but as the months dragged out, both Longfellow and Mrs. Cromer became barely tolerable. Much to the surprise of those who heard it, one of the ladies even whispered, "It's more fun watching a moth burn in the flame of a candle than listen to any more Longfellow." In the end though, Mrs. Cromer was accepted back into the fold because from time to time she would bring a wild blackberry compote that when spooned over the top of a buttery biscuit was to die for.

"Mr. Potsworth." There was a pause on Mr. Berry's part while he waited to get Edgar's attention. "How is the bookbinding business these days?"

Edgar, taking his time to reply, said with a hint of annoyance, "These days?" He shifted his seated weight with a jerk first to the left and then to the right; it would be fair to question what was gained by those sudden and jerky movements. It's uncertain as to the intentions, but for Edgar to finish with his answer he felt it was necessary to lay his fork down on the edge of his plate. Slowly looking across the table at Mr. Berry he replied, "It's been very slow!" At this moment he admitted to himself that he just felt a tinge of disdain for Berry.

The two men studied each other by fixing their eyes on one little quiddity; Edgar got the upper hand by not blinking. Mr. Berry eventually cast his eyes elsewhere, and they got back to eating.

Finally, Miss Fielders sat down and joined the group. She had come to love all of her boarders, especially Mr. Edgar Potsworth, who was a delight to be around. But she held the right to keep a close eye on him and support him through his loneliness and what she had classified as "self-loathing" moments. She was aware of his traumatic family events from when he was quite young. With her soup spoon paused, she contemplated Mr. Potsworth.

Suddenly the clatter of Edgar's dropping his fork in the middle of his plate startled everyone and caused what meager conversation there was to freeze. Edgar rose to his feet, staring at the swinging door that separated the kitchen and dining room. Who was coming through the door? His expression changed as in came the odiferous fragrance first, followed by—there she was—Miss Norma Parks.

He rapped the table with his knuckles, causing his plate to jump. "Damn, there she is and all of her stink," he whispered. But the lingering pain from rapping the table gave him enough of a pause to remember the past. Yes, the past.

Two years earlier, Norma had come waltzing through his life like she was its social director, and he'd been smitten with her. Then one morning she became a different—you could even say *strange*—person. You could smell her before she even entered the room. Her splash was atrocious, and she practically *bathed* in it. Everyone noticed this change—it was akin to smelling brimstone directly from hell. That had been the end of his smittenness.

Miss Fielders said, "Miss Parks, take a seat and I'll get you a plate so you can join us—there's plenty."

Norma sat right next to him.

Edgar struggled—should he go to his room, or remain and be the bigger person? He stayed.

While Norma was pushing her peas around on her plate, Miss Fielders asked her if she'd had the pleasure of meeting Mr. Potsworth, whom she was seated next to.

Turning in her chair and slightly leaning back for a better look, she pushed her bifocals up the bridge of her nose and said, "No."

Edgar, in an attempt to quickly bring the suffocating moment to an end, forced his introduction on her and, to cement its termination, shoved a loaded forkful of mashed potatoes into his mouth and held the clump between his tongue and the roof of his mouth.

Norma, correctly interpreting what she'd just witnessed, said, "Well!" and returned to her peas in a huff.

Miss Fielders, who didn't miss much, quickly brought to the conversation the fact that she had baked a wonderful apple pie and a rhubarb cobbler for dessert. She also announced that later that evening a Southern gentleman would be arriving. "His stay will be for several months, and I'm sure we all look forward to what he will bring to the group."

Someone asked what he did for a living and Miss Fielders said that he should be the one to answer those questions. Another boarder made a comment about the sheets being a little bit worn feeling, and she successfully shut that down: "That's office talk and not table discussion, thank you."

Mr. William Barely, who hadn't said a word all evening, coughed at the conclusion of Miss Fielders's thank-you, which he pointed out was her polite way of saying "conversation is over," and that brought a round of laughter.

Just then there was knock at the door. Miss Fielders peeked out the lace curtain that hung covering the beveled glass in the upper part of the door, then stepped back and opened the door. In walked the Southern gentleman they'd been expecting—Mr. Harold Pittman himself.

During the commotion and the rotating introductions, Edgar became subtly aware that Norma's little finger had found its way across the gap from where she sat to his leg.

Mr. Pittman said, "I'm from Savannah, Georgia. I'm a regional manager with Southern Bell Telephone preparing for the installation of dial telephones. No more listening in on other calls!" He chuckled. "Yep, party lines are about over."

Edgar was now aware that Norma's little finger was flicking a crease in his dress slacks. The remarkable aspect of this whole matter was that she looked straight ahead as though nothing were happening—or as though she did this every day with any man who sat close by.

Miss Fielders rose to her feet to take requests for either pie or cobbler. When done she said, "The count is even and that makes it easier." She came back into the dining room carrying a tray with a sterling silver pot of hot coffee and eight hand-painted, bone china cups and matching saucers. For those who wanted to "doctor up their coffee," as she would say, a shiny, sterling silver sugar bowl and matching creamer were brought in on a small silver tray.

Everyone was about settled when Mrs. Cromer, who'd disappeared while awaiting dessert, walked in with a poetry book in hand. When she smiled really big, and when the light was just right, her gold filling would sparkle.

"How darling," murmured Norma quietly so as not to be heard by anyone other than Edgar. He noticed that when she took to speaking openly, her little pinkie seemed to find a smidgen of flesh. His leg kicked, a natural reflex of pain.

Miss Fielders directed the conversation to Mr. Berry. "Mr. Berry, you were about to tell us some more about the janitorial business when Mr. Pittman knocked at the door, so please tell us about some of the challenges that you face today."

Mr. Berry, feeling a bit on the spot, stammered around.

Edgar tried to be respectful and listen carefully to each person speaking, and in doing so he lost track of what Norma was doing. Taking careful inventory of matters, he realized she had hooked her index finger through the space of his little finger and his third finger. This configuration made it possible to close her finger and hold on to his little finger. He realized immediately that this was her way of saying "we're together." Not intentionally but purely by habit, he glanced at her. Her eyes were doing the same thing those hoochie-coochie women do when trying to lure an innocent man into their web so they can eat him for dinner.

Miss Fielders kept an eye on the two lovebirds as she turned the conversation to Mr. Pittman. "If it isn't too much to share with the group, what is the process involved to go to an automatic system?"

Mr. Pittman began by stating that a new building would need to be constructed that would house the sensitive equipment, mainly "drop relays." Trunk lines would need to run from central over to the relays, passing first through manual switches that would be thrown when the sign was given—or in this situation, they might just use jumper wires instead of switches.

Norma asked, "Who gets to make the first phone call?"

A moment later, bored with the detailed description of drop relays, Edgar said to Norma, "After dessert, let's take a stroll around the block. Do you want to?"

She gazed up to the corner of the room, then answered him, "I'm a lady, so there will be no getting frisky with this lady of Victorian breeding."

Edgar stood studying her and thought about saying "forget it," but he held his tongue.

As they went out the front door, Miss Fielders said, "Bye-bye" with a "be careful" added to complete her sincerity.

The men sighed as the air cleared and they could return to breathing normally. Miss Fielders gave them a shush.

Mrs. Cromer opened up her Longfellow and commented on the titles of some poetry, in hopes someone would beg for a few verses. When that didn't happen, she slumped down in her chair and remained silent for some time. After she tired of pouting, she slammed the book shut, stalked to the door, shouted good night, and slammed the door shut too.

Miss Fielders stood with her mouth open. "What in the heck is going on with everyone?"

AT BREAKFAST THE NEXT MORNING, MISS FIELDERS HAD the table loaded to feed a small army, and everyone was counted present except for two. Lilly had come into the room with a wisp of summer morning happiness humming, "Good morning, good morning," and Mr. Pittman, the telephone system supervisor, held a clipboard at arm's length for better visibility. Mrs. Cromer sat near the end of the table, with Longfellow noticeably absent. Mr. Barely was his usual quiet self as Mr. Berry pontificated. Edgar's napkin remained next to his plate untouched, and Miss Norma Parks and her excessive use of the splash concoction were absent.

Miss Fielders puzzled out loud her concern for Mr. Potsworth and Miss Parks, but was silenced when the front door opened up unusually wide and in walked the two, shoulder to shoulder.

As they passed, everyone noticed the splash was still missing. "Hallelujah," someone said under their beath. The ones eating laid down their forks to hear the two weave the tale of where they had been since dinner last night.

Norma went first. "Honestly, I'm mortified by what Mr. Potsworth did to me after we left last night."

Someone softly gasped on hearing that.

"He was well prepared. It was premeditated, I'm telling you! He knew exactly what route to take, and we ended up at the fountain in front of the courthouse."

Another soft gasp.

"When we stopped, he turned to me and the look on his face was scary. I knew I was in trouble and cooperation was the only way to stay alive. First, he took two bars of Lava soap out of his coat pockets and told me to get down to my unmentionables. 'I'll turn my back,' he said. I started to protest but sensed that would be useless, so I did as he instructed. There I stood, practically naked, and he started scrubbing my skin. Then, having not forgotten a thing, he took a towel that was wrapped around his waist under his shirt and started drying me off. Next, he handed me another dress, neatly folded from his coat pocket, to put on."

This time instead of a gasp, the voice murmured, "How nice."

"His last act of indignity was colossally insulting: he poured out the bottle of my splash—every drop. That was when I really fell apart and cried and cried."

To add insult to injury, everyone at the table started yelling and clapping their hands. Someone even told her, "We all suffered over the stink of the splash."

Edgar reminded her to tell the rest of the story.

She was slow in getting started, but finally she did, working the story in between sobs. She concluded, still sobbing, "And we set a December wedding date."

Then things really got loud. The women squealed with joy (mostly for Edgar) and Mr. Berry was overheard saying, "Oh my gosh, how sickening—has everyone forgotten her stink?"

Mrs. Cromer chimed in, "Well, she got her splash after all—water."

✦

THE MANICURE

CHANCE BOATWRIGHT SAT ON THE CURB THINKING about how his life had fallen apart in such a big way. To begin with, his wife had left him. To make matters worse, he'd just been laid off as the top welder for McCall's Boat Works in Newport News, Virginia, where he'd worked for the past twelve years. As he sat trying to piece together his future, he couldn't help but study his rough hands and the calluses on them. His wife had up and run off with another man, whom she'd described as gentle, thoughtful, but most of all loving, and with the softest hands one could imagine for a man. As it turned out, he was an executive with McCall's; she'd met him at a company picnic three years earlier.

The blast of a car horn brought him back to the moment, but he finished the thought: *She's going to be sorry for what she's done to me.*

His friend Will Goble gave him a ride to and from work each day. Few words were exchanged when he got in the car.

"Stop the car. Stop now," Chance suddenly demanded. "There she is with him. The bastard that stole my wife and broke up our home."

Will, seeing Chance's wife for the first time said, "She's a real looker. But, Chance, he didn't break up your home. Your wife would have fancied anyone who came along. For whatever reason she wasn't happy. She was on the hunt."

"Yeah, yeah, I know, I know. What a pile of shit this is."

"How about a beer, buddy?"

"No, no, no," Chance said, with the last no not sounding too sure.

"Let's stop here at Beer and Nuts. Not a very alluring name, is it?"

Inside, the bartender, a well-developed woman in her late forties, said, "Gents, what will it be tonight?"

Will spoke first. "Give us two draft specials and two boats of nuts, Billye Ra." After she had served them, Will laid down a five-dollar bill and thanked her. The conversation was short with Billye Ra—she was too busy primping every time she walked past the mirror on the wall behind the bar.

After they'd ordered their third drink, Billye Ra mentioned to them that this was her last night. Chance perked up. He asked who the owner was and Billye Ra pointed at a man across the room. "Russell."

Chance spoke to Russell immediately and snagged the job before another Billye Ra came in with her shirt tail tied in a knot and the top two buttons undone. Chance knew all along that this would be temporary until he could find a better-paying job—one where didn't have to deal with drunks and deadbeats. But it would do for now.

After a week he received his first paycheck, and he knew exactly how he was going to spend part of the money.

Before going out that morning, he washed his hands thoroughly and with an old cloth he cleaned up his shoes. His first stop was at a fancy salon. When he entered, he could tell right away that he was not the type of patron one would expect to see there. The woman working there was very elegant with her hair done up in fancy swirls, light blue eyeshadow, and lipstick that reminded him of the original paint job on the new wagon he got when he was a little kid.

He was about ready to turn and walk out when the woman came to him and said, "Sir, what can we do for you?"

Before he got the answer out, he was struck by the fragrance of her cologne. It smelled like the flowers at a funeral for someone important.

She repeated her question. "How may I help you?"

Nervously, he spoke in a voice barely loud enough for her to hear him. "I would like a man-a-kure. You know, a nail job. And something to make my hands really soft. Can you do all that for me?"

She directed him to a small table and got him a chair that seemed too small for his build. A young woman came and sat down on the opposite side of the table, placing a small bowl of warm soapy water between them. Carefully she lifted his massive rough hands and led his fingertips to the bowl.

"You just let those fingertips get soft," she said, "and then I'll be back."

After she trimmed his fingernails and cuticles, she took a pumice stone to the rough areas of his hands. Chance thought it looked like a lava rock.

She said, "Chance, that's the best I can do at this time, but you can come back tomorrow, and I can work a little more on the calluses."

Just as Chance was getting up from the small table, the door to his right and slightly behind him opened. Without looking, he recognized his wife's voice as she was talking to a man. He didn't want to be seen, so he stayed partly bent over and shuffled his feet to the right, trying to be inconspicuous. Outside, he hustled to the corner, turned, and headed to his apartment.

As he walked home, he kept admiring his hands, feeling one and then the other, and then looking carefully, first at the knuckles and then at the palms. He smiled and felt that maybe, just maybe, Marilyn would approve. But that was in the past. It was too late for that now. His mind quickly jumped to hurting Marilyn for cheating on him. He ended the mental exercise with one word: *Slut.*

The close call had made him sweat and with the chill in the air it was a cool walk home. Chance had a lot of time to consider his many problems. Unfortunately, the longer he walked, the more he thought, and the more he thought, the angrier he became. Finally, he reached his apartment. He'd settled down a little bit, but not enough to take the taste of anger, resentment, and hate from his mouth. He paused and thought that different feelings really do taste different. But he also realized that it was the genesis of the feeling that governed the taste. Three of the biggest events in life are the loss of a job, the loss of a spouse, and death; he'd experienced two of the three. *But she's going to experience the third one.*

IT WAS 9 P.M. AND TIME TO HEAD TO WORK. ALONG THE way, Chance decided that tomorrow during the day he would set out and search for better employment. When he arrived at Beer and Nuts, the place was packed and loud. Packed was good because he made more tips, but loud was something that got old real fast. Packed also meant arguments between drunks; eventually a fight would break out and he'd have to intervene before they tore the place up, and that usually involved catching a wild fist in the mouth. He cussed at the thought of finding another job.

That night he had a wild dream about his wife and the executive. During the dream, the hurt and anguish were terrible. He woke up sweating and thrashing around in the bed. His sheet and pillow were on the floor, and the lampshade by his bed was damaged.

The next morning, he felt like he hadn't rested at all. He felt like he was boxed in, with no direction to go that would alleviate his hurt and pain. The one answer that continued to come at him again and again was to hurt Marilyn. Maybe take out the executive and let her hurt over his death. Almost immediately he felt regret for his savage thinking. Nonetheless, he was hurting, and that hurt needed a form of relief, and he knew of only one way. It was strange and incongruent, but he remembered that one summer at a bible study his mother had put to him the discussion of atonement, how Christ had paid for our sins. Chance's big hand was on a small plastic ashtray at the bar, and suddenly the thing crumbled under his powerful grip. Without paying much attention, he pulled a sliver from his hand and walked the full length of the bar to tell a couple of guys to knock off the foul talk.

Once he closed up the bar, he took his time walking home, because he wanted an answer before he arrived at his apartment. How could he get even with his wife and her lover at the same time? He got to his place before he had the answer that he was searching for, so he took a seat on the front stoop. He was about to light up his second cigarette when he heard his wife's voice and a man's voice coming towards him. He didn't want them to find him sitting there like a deadbeat, but there wasn't enough time to duck inside. He stuck the unlit cigarette into his coat pocket and laid his forehead on his arms across his knees. He listened to their footsteps as they walked past him without even hesitating for a closer look.

Once he was sure that they had passed, he carefully rolled his head over to sneak a peek. What he saw made him jerk upright and really look. It was his wife but not the executive. She had her arm through the man's arm. Chance thought the man's frame looked a little familiar, but it was dark. Wait a minute, what was going on here?

And the solution came to him in a flash. A lover's triangle. *Yes, that's it. You just have to be patient, and the answer will fall in your lap. Let me piece this together . . . The executive sees Marilyn with another man, he becomes jealous, and he kills Marilyn for double-timing him. Sure, that will work perfectly. Who's going to care about some broad getting it for cheating anyhow?*

Chance stayed up late that night working out the details so things would go as planned and the executive would get the blame. The no-good wife stealer.

Early the next morning before sunup, Chance quietly left his apartment. He left the kitchenette light on and had a pot of coffee ready to brew on the stove burner the minute he walked back in the door.

He stood in front of Marilyn's house, terrified. He was about to kill a person. His plans were to stab her with a knife and cut up her face to make it look like an angry love affair gone bad. He went to the back of the house, where he knew a window was always open. He tried to use his big knife to pry open the window, but it wouldn't move.

"Damn," he said under his breath.

He went to the window on the other side of the steps. It slid up with ease. He carefully crawled through. Once in, he removed his shoes to be quieter as he moved to the bedroom.

He stood at the closed bedroom door. He reached for the knob and turned it slowly. Gently he pushed the door open a sliver and heard sounds on the other side. The room was dark. He heard a man's voice, then a woman crying. Chance froze. He needed time to think. Two people to deal with at one time, not good at all. He stood for what seemed the longest time. He wiped the sweat from his brow. His stomach was churning. Thoughts of backing out ran through his mind. He turned to leave and try another day, but then decided now was the time. Almost on impulse, he charged into the room with a kind of battle cry, as if to draw courage from the sound.

He went for the man. *Take the biggest one down first.* As he went around the foot of the bed, he dragged the blanket up and threw it over the man's head. Then he drove the knife home.

His wife screamed and headed for the door. Chance reached out and grabbed her by the wrist. She fell backwards on the bed and lay there naked. He looked long and hard into her eyes and saw terror. Chance could tell by her struggle to talk and the pleading look in her eyes that she wanted to say she was sorry. But the words would never come forth. Chance shoved the knife that was in her rib cage further up into her heart.

He checked to make sure they both were dead. *Yes.*

He left the house and was just about to go around to the front when he felt dampness on his feet. Morning dew. In the height of the moment, he'd forgotten his shoes. He returned to the back window, but this time when he left, he went out the back door. With shoes on, he walked casually down the sidewalk to his apartment. As he passed by some brackish runoff from the ocean, he wiped the knife clean of prints and tossed it into the water.

CHANCE READ THE PAPER CAREFULLY THE NEXT FEW days. In the articles about the crime, neighbors reported

Marilyn had men coming and going at different times of the day and night. He was pleased to read the comments, which helped make it look like some jealous lover had decided to end the affairs this woman was having. He relaxed.

Three days after the murder, the police reported a suspect was in hand. Chance wondered who it could be.

The next day the paper named the suspect: Will Goble.

Damn, my best friend was sleeping with my wife. That's the body frame I saw that dark night walking with her.

Chance let the paper slip from his hands to the floor. He was sick to his stomach.

When the trial was held, Will was convicted on two counts of first-degree murder. Again, Chance was sickened because he knew Will was innocent. For days he moped around knowing that an innocent man was going to the electric chair for something that he himself had done.

After a week of not sleeping and days of worry about letting his friend pay for what he had done, it was becoming more than he could tolerate.

Exhausted and out of strength and energy, he took one long last look around his apartment, walked out, and closed the door knowing he would never see it again. But instead of turning to the right towards the police station, he went to the left and headed to the manicurist. He wanted his hands to feel soft and his nails and cuticles to look like a gentleman's while in the chair.

✦

OTTO AND MARJORIE GO TO YELLOWSTONE

"WELL," MARJORIE SAID TO OTTO, "I SURE hope you enjoy this trip and act in a manner that won't embarrass us to tears." She prodded Otto to get aboard the train by pointing her little suitcase in the direction of the porter tearing tickets.

Otto had never been on a train and neither had Marjorie. She knew she needed to keep a short rein on Otto and headed in the general direction of Wyoming. Otto plopped down in the first seat that suited his fancy.

Marjorie was quick to notice the early infraction. "Otto, please, let's work together on this trip."

Otto said, "Marjorie, I am well aware of the importance of this trip regarding your well-being and getting some much-needed rest, and I intend to make that happen for you!"

Otto was slow in moving up three rows.

Marjorie said, "This will be a mighty long trip."

Once Otto found the correct seat and sat down, he got out a sandwich and started eating while the train was still parked at the station.

Marjorie said, "That's your dinner for tonight that you're eating at noon, did you know that?"

"Yow, now that you told me I do."

"Now, Otto, listen to me. Ask before you take and before you speak, *please*."

Otto was quick with an answer. "There is that please again—it gets me every time!" After a pause Otto asked, "Marjorie, did you lock up the house?"

"Why would we lock up? What is it that we have that's worth keeping?"

Otto, a little defensively, said, "Marjorie, we have some personal items that should remain private."

"Otto, don't get so rankled over silly stuff. The one thing that should remain private is the number of holes in your long johns—and I don't mean the ones for your arms, neck, and rear end."

"Oh."

"Take a nap, young man," she snapped.

When she heard Otto snoring, Marjorie relaxed some, but not for long.

Otto started talking in his sleep, and then his snoring became louder and louder, but she was most disturbed when he really became himself while sleeping and broke wind.

She gave him an elbow in the ribs, which was enough to make him sit up. She whispered, "Do you know what 'uncouth' means?"

"No, and I don't want to know. I want to sleep."

"Well, that explains so much," she said as she tried to get comfortable.

He quickly sat up. "Marjorie, does it have something to do with a cougar?"

"Enjoy your sleep," she said.

OTTO WAS ENJOYING HIS LIVERWURST SANDWICH WHILE Marjorie talked to a woman seated across the aisle. He nudged Marjorie to tell her that the coffee was still hot and that the thermos was a good idea. Marjorie prayed he would not let go of a loud burp when finished. She deliberately didn't put onions on for that very reason.

The train jolted forward.

"On to Kansas City!" said Otto, but quickly realized he was talking to himself; Marjorie was busy talking to the woman seated next to her.

Otto got tired staring out the window, so he got up and headed in the direction of the engine. "I'm lonely," he muttered. He glanced back at Marjorie and mumbled to himself, "She sure is a gadabout." He found it hard to not bump into the back of seats because of the rocking movement of the train. Each time he bumped someone, he stopped to apologize. He bumped into one seat where two gentlemen were seated, and that got a conversation started. The older of the two suggested that they go to the front of this car where there were seats facing each other; there they could talk more freely and comfortably.

After they were all seated, the older man suggested a

friendly game of cards. At that same time, the conductor came through collecting their tickets. Otto noticed each man had a tiny pocket above the larger one on his coat. The man saw Otto looking and told him it was called a ticket pocket.

"The suit I'm wearing is a bespoke suit," the man said.

Otto, not to be outdone on pockets, retrieved his ticket from a top pocket on his bib overalls. He couldn't help but notice the man's fine dress attire: his brown suit, ecru shirt, and brown and white geometric design tie. Otto dreamed of such a look; he knew this man visited the best haberdasheries in the big cities. He wanted to get Marjorie to show her, but he knew better.

Otto was not familiar with any card games and thought his lack of skill would be a distraction to the group.

"We'll make it easy on all of us," the older gent said. "I know an easy card game, simple poker. Each man gets two cards and whoever has the best hand wins."

Well, Otto thought, *that sounds easy enough.*

The game continued for nearly three hours and Otto was in debt for almost two thousand dollars when Marjorie walked up and saw the most reckless thing Otto could have gotten involved in. She gave Otto a firm back-of-her-hand slap on his shoulder to move over so she could park her backside.

"Now, I don't know any of you men and quite frankly I don't want to know you, but let me tell you what has happened here and then I'm going to tell you what happens next. Here it is, men: you knew in the very beginning that this man," she rested her hand on Otto's shoulder signaling support, "was boondoggled into this game not knowing what he was doing. He knew nothing about card games. Gentlemen, now be honest: I'm right, aren't I?"

With hesitation each man grudgingly gave in and answered, "Yes."

"Otto, pick up your money on the table."

Both men became agitated and said he didn't have any money on the table.

"Well, Otto, do you have any of their money in your pockets?"

He nodded his head yes.

"Give it back to them."

He complied.

"As it stands now, Otto doesn't have any of your money, right?"

The two men said yes.

"But you have signed IOUs from Otto, right?"

"Right," they said.

"Fork 'em over."

The men took the IOUs in sum of two thousand dollars from their pockets and handed them to Marjorie.

"Now, fellows, this is a biggie for you: do you have any more?"

No, loud and clear, was their answer.

"Men, you have been gentlemen, but you are crooks dressed in gentlemen's clothes. What car should you be in?"

"This car."

"Otto, let's go to our car."

Marjorie took her time in getting up, which allowed her time to collect her words. "Men, you are damn lucky that I didn't grab each one of you little bits and pull you across the booth table and shake you until your eyes popped out. We will not see you again, right?" She picked up a wooden matchstick from the table and gripped it so part of it stuck out slightly above her clenched fist. Using her thumb, she broke off the top. "This was how close you two were to death tonight."

When she and Otto got back to their seats, they found two men sitting there.

"Listen, you hayseeds. My man and I were seated here before you two sashayed up and parked your hindquarters. I hope we're going to do this polite-like, or am I going to send you skunks to the engine room as fuel?"

In the twinkle of an eye, they were up and gone!

"Something else, Otto. Sit square on your rump and when you fall asleep, don't lean over; remain upright. Maybe that will stop you from passing gas."

Otto just smiled real big inside, proud that Marjorie took tough matters in hand.

THE TRAIN CAME TO AN ABRUPT HALT, WHICH SHOOK everyone either awake or aware. In any case, Otto sat up sputtering and stuttering. "What's wrong? Why have we stopped? Are we at Yellowstone?"

Marjorie finally got his attention. "Otto, we're stopping to take on more water and coal. This is going to be a long climb up the mountain range. Before you ask, it's never happened."

Otto asked, "What was I going to say?"

"You were going to ask whether a train has ever slid back down the tracks, and the answer is no!"

"Oh, Mr. Conductor, has the train ever slid back down backwards?" Otto asked.

"No, never!"

Marjorie just smiled and said nothing.

Otto became restless and got up for a gentleman's stroll.

Behind him Marjorie said, "Think, just think, before you do or say."

Otto was quick on his feet and turned, but instead of speaking, he just stood there and stared at Marjorie.

Finally, she said, "Otto, what in heaven's name are you doing?"

"Marjorie, you said to think before you do or say, and that is what I just did. I was going to tell you how much I love you, and then remembered, 'Think.' So, I did think and now I've decided not to say it to you!"

"Oh, Otto," she said. "Don't be mean."

Later that day, Otto stood on the conductor's platform looking up the track and back down the track where they had just come from. He could see both ways due to a long curve. Then the tracks straightened out and became flat at the same time. From the same platform, he could see the hitch pin that connected the two cars together. He also noticed that as the slack between the cars changed, the pin seemed to just float in the hole at times.

Otto struggled with the temptation to lift the pin up and out just to see if he could then drop it back in before the slack changed. Marjorie's words haunted him, "Think before you do or say."

It was too late: the pin was out, and the distance continued to grow between the two cars. Otto was sweating and scared. He wished Marjorie were there.

Then the grade must have changed because the cars were reversing their course; they were getting close again.

No, now they were going in the wrong direction—they were getting farther apart.

Oh, why did I take that stupid pin out anyway?

Otto got down on his hands and knees to be ready to drop the pin in the two holes once they lined up.

Now he was on his belly, hanging over just a little, ready to undo his wrong.

"Come on. Just a little more. Come on, you bugger, just a bit. Oooh now!" And he let go of the pin and the sound of the metals clinking was more pleasurable than he could take.

There! He was worn out, so he settled back on his rear, legs spread straight out and apart, and breathed heavily.

"Otto, what in heaven's sake are you doing?" Marjorie stood over him with her hands on her hips waiting for an answer.

"Nothing."

"Are you thinking before doing, Otto?"

Let it pass, he thought.

AFTER HOURS AND HOURS OF TRAVELING THROUGH THE night, the train pulled into the station in Wyoming. Otto was first in gathering different pieces of luggage and his bag of snacks that included one sandwich. Now the journey would continue by bus. Excitedly, Otto nudged Marjorie to tell her that they had arrived.

Marjorie said, "Arrived where? The home where we'll put you, or what?"

"No, sweet pumpkin, the train depot. We'll travel the rest of the way by bus. They don't allow trains in the park."

Once they got to the park, Otto stood in the main lodge, mesmerized by its construction. The ceiling joists were as big around as a man's waist. *Not mine*, he thought, and a tinge of regret crossed his mind. The ceiling's knotty pine boards were evenly covered with smoke stains from the walk-in fireplace. Otto saw animals stuffed and mounted for display hanging on the walls. He had no clue what some of them were. He carefully mumbled to himself that one looked like someone from Marjorie's family, and about that same time Marjorie came up real close to him. He thought he had been caught.

Then she said, "Otto, I feel like this is one of your family reunions." She laughed and poked him in the ribs.

With key in hand, they walked the carpeted hallway to their room. The carpet had different scenes woven into it; Otto stayed busy looking to see which scene repeated itself. He liked the herd of buffalos, and the one of the Tetons—he swore that one was his favorite—but then he saw Old Faithful and the contest was over.

The meals in the lodge were delicious, but Otto and Marjorie thought the pies left a lot to be desired. The desk clerk and the attendants seemed to cater to them as if they knew who they were.

Marjorie said, "This is living, isn't it, Otto?"

Otto eagerly agreed.

Marjorie thought it real strange that Hershel should pop into her mind. Hershel was the undertaker from back home who took care of burying people from the mountain. But she had not been feeling her old energetic self lately and she'd been feeling worse and worse as the trip continued. She experienced a cold chill and shiver and then dismissed it all as nonsense. She remembered this trip was all about her getting some rest and recuperation since her health had declined some over the past several months. She sighed and confessed to Otto that the pie business was stressful and took more out of her than she had thought. But now she was getting tired from the walking and not being in her own home and bed.

SEVERAL DAYS HAD PASSED AND THE TRIP TO THE PARK was coming to an end. Otto had had the time of his life. He couldn't stop talking about the wildlife and how much bigger the deer were here than back home; Marjorie tried to tell him that what he thought was a deer was really an elk. Otto was in an arena where he didn't stand a chance.

"It's not a deer; it's an elk." Next, they will tell me the train is really an iron horse. And Marjorie is not helping—she's part of the problem. What can I do? I should have stayed home! Otto felt out of sorts since Marjorie was not eager to walk around much.

They decided to sit and talk about what they had seen,

how they missed the kids back home, and the blessing of their businesses. Marjorie recalled how on the first morning they had stood for hours watching Old Faithful spew water into the air. Otto's thrill was in timing the sequences. He couldn't get the image out of his mind. Otto was quick to point out that it was not as predictable as stated in the brochures. But Marjorie had gotten tired of walking so much and had returned to the lodge without Otto. Otto had continued walking on to the Grand Prismatic Spring that was enormous in size and depth. Otto felt uncomfortable with the near-boiling temperature of the springs, but he was happy to hear that the animals instinctively knew not to get too close. Marjorie and Otto remembered seeing wild buffalo and the moose and the mountain goats, but best of all they enjoyed the relaxation and just not worrying about anything.

That final night at the lodge there was a banquet for several different groups, the lodge's way of saying thanks to their guests before they departed. Otto and Marjorie decided to go for a little while, but then rest was needed.

THE MORNING FOR DEPARTURE HAD COME AND OTTO stood with suitcases out front of the lodge, waiting for Marjorie and the bus to arrive. The bus would take them back to catch the train. *I'll be glad to get back home,* he thought. *Here comes the bus and no Marjorie. Where is she?* The suitcases were being loaded on the bus, and at last Marjorie came out the front doors, but Otto thought she didn't look quite right.

As Marjorie boarded the bus, Otto noticed she looked all sweaty and pale. He calmly asked her, "What is it?"

"I don't know," she said.

"Should we stay and get a doctor here before we go on?"

Marjorie didn't manage to answer before passing out.

The hotel doctor, along with some attendants, helped to get Marjorie to a room, and someone managed to retrieve the luggage. The doctor spent an hour with her before he called for Otto to come on into the room.

The doctor looked Otto in the eye and said, "It's not serious, but the ramifications are not good."

Otto sat and muttered, "Ramifications? What's a ramification anyway?" His frown and the scared look written on his face made it look like he was the sick one.

The doctor, eager to put him out of his misery, said, "Listen, Otto, your wife is expecting a baby, and she's not doing too good with this one."

Otto said, "Well, Doc, she's had eight others and knows exactly what she needs to do."

"That's the problem—she's had too many. Her body is worn out and mentally she is worn out."

"Doc, what do you suggest we do?"

"Well, there is not a hospital up here, and the ride back on the bus and train would be too much. Can you drive?"

Otto said, "Why, yes, I can drive, but I don't have a car with me."

"Yes, yes, I know, but you can rent one, can't you?" asked the Doc.

"Well, sure I can." Otto's nervousness caused him to be a little awkward and not sure-footed. "Maybe a little assistance would be nice."

The doctor said, "Yes, we will assist you."

They spent another night in the lodge so Marjorie could rest and the doctor could check on her in the morning. Otto slept in a big lounge chair in the room so Marjorie could relax in the bed peacefully without being subjected to Otto's tossing and turning.

In the morning, Otto quietly slipped out and got them coffee and scrambled eggs and toast for breakfast. Marjorie looked better and was able to eat her breakfast. Otto was happy with her improvement. The doctor stopped by as promised and thought Marjorie was up for traveling.

The doctor said, "Otto, I have an idea that just might be the answer for your situation. My friend and patient for years now is headed up to your neck of the woods because he has some business in the area. He is willing to take the two of you to your house, for the cost of the car rental. I really think that would be easy on you both. So, what do you think?"

Otto looked to Marjorie. She gave a nod, and the deal was settled.

The doctor said, "His name is Paul Farthing, and he will meet you in the lobby at seven in the morning. Marjorie, when you get home, I want you to see your doctor immediately—and I do mean immediately—and no strenuous activity. Good luck!"

Otto sat in the big chair that night and listened to the noises of the wild. One beast in particular must have been that overgrown deer, he concluded.

The following morning, Otto and Marjorie waited for Paul in front of the lodge with suitcases lined up, showing organization and readiness. Pleasantries were exchanged, the car was loaded, and off they went.

Two days later, they pulled up to their house, and out came a small army of children to greet them. Paul was almost speechless at the sight.

Marjorie said, "Paul, I'll not take no for answer. Get down and come in and enjoy some mountain hospitality—and we need to pay you too. I'll have a fire going in this here stove before a skunk could put off stink."

Paul chuckled. "Okay."

Otto came in and said, "The boys have gone after the doc, so put out another plate and rest."

The doctor finally showed up in time to sit down for some cornbread and butterbeans with fried ham. The aroma of hot coffee and being home was better than any geyser. Marjorie had two dozen hot turnovers on a plate in the middle of the table in no time. Mostly little hands were grabbing them, but Otto and Paul had a fair share too.

"Paul, here is your money, and I'm packing some ham sandwiches along with some turnovers for your trip home. We were not told beforehand that you made this trip just to bring us home. So, I doubled the pay and added some more just for fun. I wish you would spend the night—we have plenty of room."

Paul quickly said no, and with that, he rose from the table.

MARJORIE SLEPT WELL THAT NIGHT AND WAS UP EARLY the next morning, attending to the family as usual. A knock at the door was the doctor, coming to check on her.

At long last, he came out of the room where Marjorie was and said to Otto, "I don't like this one bit, Otto. I think she may not make it through this period."

The word "period" scared Otto.

The doc continued once he had Otto's full attention. "Her vitals are very weak, but worse is her attitude. She's not her fighting self anymore. Otto, I would not mention this to the kids just yet, but I would prepare myself for the worst if I were you. The next three days will tell it all, so why is she cooking and who knows what else? She needs rest, rest, and more rest!"

Otto quietly slipped off into the living room, where he sat staring off at nothing. He was not used to these thoughts and feelings; in fact, he was in a borderline panic, and he didn't know how to handle it.

The doc had never seen Otto like this. He took Otto's hand and right away felt how cold it was; he knew Otto was in shock. "Otto, I know this has upset you tremendously, but you need to pull yourself together and be strong for the sake of the children."

Otto nodded his head like he understood, but the doctor wasn't sure he did. The doc thought, *Now I have two patients.*

The doctor summoned a younger child and asked him to go fetch Prudy, a doctor of psychology who was married to Otto and Marjorie's oldest son. The boy tore out the screened door, and in no time they both returned, worry on their faces. Prudy was eager to be of help in any way.

The doctor slid up in his chair and looked at Prudy. He went over Marjorie's conditions and then Otto's. He gave her the pillboxes he had prescribed for each patient and as a courtesy he asked her if she agreed with his diagnosis and prescriptions.

Prudy agreed, with one small question. "If Otto is in shock, should he be given a sleeping pill so soon?"

The doctor leaned back in his chair and stroked his face as a ritual to spur on the best answer. "Why, Prudy, that's a good question. What are your recommendations?"

Prudy leaned forward and said, "I'd wait until the morning. I think the stressful events here will make him welcome sleep."

"I concur, Doctor. Send for me if conditions change. I will swing by in the morning, if that's alright with you."

"Sure," she said.

The doctor sat in his buggy and smiled thinking how long it had been since he'd left two patients and felt this at peace. They were in good hands. With an even bigger smile, he gave Ole Fanny a swat on her rump with his whip and off they went. The doctor's means were meager since most of his patients paid him with farm products or invitations to a meal, but he declared himself rich to have Ole Fanny.

Later that night the doctor sat at home in his overstuffed leather chair reading a medical book on sedatives and was again proud of Prudy and how she was right on with her diagnosis and recommendation about the use of sedatives. This mountain would benefit in keeping her here, if she would stay. The leather chair was too comfortable for such a tired body and mind. He had fallen asleep here many times and he did so again that night, a deep sleep.

AT ABOUT 2 A.M., THE DOCTOR WAS AWAKENED BY A banging at his door. On the other side stood a young boy he didn't recognize, one who was frantic with tears running down his cheeks.

"Come quick," he said. "Miss Marjorie is dead."

The doc felt a sudden weakness in his knees and a brief moment of confusion, and the sadness was overwhelming! He had come to love so many of these people on the mountain and Marjorie was at the very top—she was a special lady. Doc figured that she must have hemorrhaged in the night.

Otto was a mess; it took a strong sedative to get him settled down.

Prudy, along with the help of the older children, fixed dinner for everyone. But Otto would have nothing to do with a meal. He did get the jug of moonshine out of the cupboard though.

Doc was annoyed by someone pulling on his arm saying the words over and over, "Wake up. Wake up, Doc. Come on, Doc. Marjorie is asking for you to come, so please."

Doc sat up in his chair feeling like he had been drugged but realized that it was a matter of fatigue and exhaustion. He stumbled to the water basin and splashed water on his face, which brought him to the point of comprehension.

Thank God it was a bad dream.

"Yes, let's get going," he said.

WHEN THE DOCTOR ARRIVED, PRUDY WAS SEATED WITH a gentleman who introduced himself as Mr. Cooksey. Mr.

Cooksey had apparently arranged the deal that had put Marjorie's pies all over America. Puzzled, Doc listened to Mr. Cooksey babble on as he wondered where Marjorie and Otto were.

Mr. Cooksey said, "Well, I must tell you, Mrs. Simms is a good businesswoman. Is Mr. Simms here? He is going to love what she did just before they went to Yellowstone. She sold the recipe and all the techniques for baking the best turnovers we have ever eaten, and I came by to drop off his first check and get the address for his bank."

The looks on Prudy's and Doc's faces were of unmistakable surprise.

Mr. Cooksey stopped mid-sentence. "What's up? She put it all in Mr. Simms's name and formed a company. She wanted Otto to have the same type of personal ownership in his company as she had in the pie business."

From the back bedroom came a strong voice, not to be confused with anyone else. "Otto, are you up? If not, why not? And why did you let me sleep so late anyway?"

Otto followed Marjorie out from the back, scratching.

"Ah, there you are. Shall we get started?" said Mr. Cooksey.

With Otto and Marjorie seated, Mr. Cooksey took control of the meeting and in no time, he was thanking all for attending. He presented Otto with his first check.

Otto looked the check over from one edge to the other edge and smiled. "Marjorie, do you know what this means? I'm a potentate just like you are. That's funny, huh?"

He rose up to give Marjorie a kiss on the cheek.

"You're a pootentate alright, Otto," she said with a hint of sarcasm.

They both laughed.

Otto and the kids went into the kitchen to fix turnovers and coffee for everyone while the doc helped Marjorie back to her bedroom.

When Doc returned, Otto asked, "Honestly, is she going to make it?"

Doc stroked his face again as he decided on what answer to give Otto. "If she will stay in that bed and you and the kids can leave her alone—don't let her do a thing—she may pull through this. I'm not sure."

With that piece of good news, Otto was in a great mood and started barking orders at the kids to leave Momma alone. "No one for any reason is to go near her bedroom door! Now, you little skitters, get into the kitchen and clean 'er up. Get her shining like a diamond in a . . ."

Marjorie shouted, "Otto!"

He smiled.

✦

RENA'S MERRY CHRISTMAS

RENA WAS A YOUNG IMMIGRANT FROM A SMALL village five kilometers north of Rome. She had traveled to the Americas with her mama and papa, who were rounded up shortly after arriving at Staten Island and returned to Italy. There was little help available then for immigrants, especially poor ones. She was all alone except for the harsh and unsympathetic New York immigration authorities working with the Port Authority officers, who immediately placed her in an orphanage anticipating a quick adoption. It was the middle of the twentieth century, and life overwhelmed Rena. The sights and sounds were so different from what she was accustomed to that most of the time she was bewildered.

Several months passed and she remained in the orphanage receiving little attention. What attention she did receive was not loving or affectionate but gruff and harsh. Her meals were mainly thin soups twice a day and oatmeal for breakfast, which was a bit more substantial. The bread was stale and tasteless but was offered with each meal. The water was plentiful—but not for bathing or general handwashing, just for drinking. Rena never saw any of the kids, young or old, leave with an adult couple, but several left on cots with wheels, and when they did, she never saw them around again.

ACROSS TOWN A YOUNG MARRIED COUPLE STOOD BEFORE a judge, pleading to adopt a little girl from the orphanage. The judge reminded them they were not following the proper procedures for adopting a child.

"What's more important—rules and procedures, or a child getting a nice home with loving parents?" pleaded the woman.

"Mrs. Pernell," said the judge, "I will give you an answer tomorrow. Come back at 11 a.m."

THAT NIGHT AT THE ORPHANAGE RENA SLEPT BETWEEN two younger girls. She remembered her mama saying, "We survive by getting, but true living comes from giving." Her mother reminded her over and over that some important man named Winston Churchill had said that—or at least something like that. Rena made it her motto, and from that night on she looked after the two girls. Before she went to sleep, she lay awake dreaming about playing the piano. Back in Italy, her neighbor, Maria Reggie, had given her piano lessons in exchange for Rena's sweeping and mopping her floor each week. Mrs. Reggie had told her she had a special talent and shouldn't waste it. But now Rena didn't have a piano to practice on.

MRS. PERNELL AND HER HUSBAND LEFT THE COURTROOM smiling so big that people stared at them, trying to figure out what had happened. Linda and William Pernell were now parents. They were so elated that when the first five cabs failed to stop for them, they laughed.

When they finally got a cab, it drove them to the orphanage to pick up Rena, whom they'd chosen the prior week. Every time a car got in front of them, Mrs. Pernell's excitement and impatience would cause her to tell the driver to move over, please.

Finally, the Pernells walked out of the orphanage holding their daughter's hand. What a proud moment. With parenthood came responsibilities; it was shopping time.

THE PERNELLS WERE PERFECT PARENTS TO RENA. SHE never wanted for anything, including love and affection. She was enrolled at the best private schools and wore the current fashions. The years flew by and eventually she started thinking about life and what she needed to prepare for in the future. William had been promoted to bank president and Linda had become a successful display designer for a large jewelry store on Fifth Avenue. Rena blossomed into an outstanding young lady. She attended Our Lady of Sorrows Convent and earned high marks that might lead her into a good college there in the North.

Rena had many interests as young people do, but one day she decided to rekindle what at one time had been a passion for the piano. She also remembered that she had caught on quickly. As a child, learning had felt effortless for her, and she had quickly become proficient at playing almost any music put before her. She was excited about this idea and found it harder to sleep each night. One day Rena woke up and realized she had discovered exactly what she wanted to do with her life: she wanted to become a famous pianist. She quickly corrected "famous" to "outstanding." She wanted to be someone who was well trained and had serious, flawless application.

What Rena *really* had in mind was getting herself in a position where she could get her parents back to the US so she could take care of them. She studied hard and practiced even harder because she was determined to see them again.

The Pernells came to see her often at school. Mrs. Pernell missed Rena very much; Mr. Pernell was more serious and less emotional. Rena wanted to tell them of her future goals in helping her mama and papa return to this country, but she was worried that such a discussion would hurt the Pernells' feelings. But she knew it needed to be done because she was eager to share her desires.

Rena squirmed in her seat and turned to her mom. "Mom and Dad, there is something I want to tell you two."

No sooner had those words cleared Rena's lips than her mother said, "Oh, William, look at the time. I have the appointment with Mr. Brooks in thirty minutes. We need to go now."

She quickly rose to her feet and leaned down to give Rena a kiss on her cheek, leaving an imprint of red lipstick.

Rena's blank expression said it all as she was left to sit and watch them walk off, listening to the click, click, click of her mother's high heels as she walked down the hallway.

"Dismissed, but not defeated," she mumbled to herself. A powerful emotion swept over Rena. *I'm going to get my mama and papa here if it's the last thing I do!*

Rena hired a personal tutor named Ellie McPerson to teach her the piano. Rena relearned the basics and started progressing so rapidly that Ellie couldn't believe it. Rena had a natural sense of rhythm—she had already learned the concept of soul.

Rena had been at it for four short months, and she was already begging for a solo show. Quite frankly, Ellie couldn't come up with a valid reason to say no—Rena was that proficient on the keyboard. Rena began playing in orchestras as a fill-in when someone was sick or away, but it wasn't long before she became a regular performer in some very grand places and sometimes even soloed.

THROUGH HER PERFORMING, RENA BECAME QUITE WELL off financially, so she hired Walt Chaney, a private investigator who was known for tracking people down all over the world. She spent an entire afternoon with Walt, describing in detail traits of her mama and papa: foods they loved, hobbies, music, and a whole myriad of normal and unusual interests. She gave him a dozen photos that her mama had put in her valise when they first came to America.

Rena's musical skill level had outgrown Ellie's ability, and Ellie sadly told Rena that she would need to work with another instructor. Ellie gave her the name of Terrance Weston, who she thought could take Rena to higher levels. Rena was sad but at the same time excited about the opportunity to learn new techniques.

RENA HAD JUST RETURNED FROM VISITING WITH HER mom and dad, which she always enjoyed, but she had lost time at the keyboard working with Mr. Weston. Her parents were only somewhat interested in her piano playing, so she didn't share much with them. She was hurriedly going through some stacked-up mail and there was a letter from Mr. Chaney regarding her mama and papa in Italy.

> *Miss Rena,*
>
> *It has been an exhausting trip abroad with some small successes but with larger losses. I'm afraid that the advance you so eagerly gave me has run out. If you want me to continue my work, regrettably I must inform you that more funds are needed.*
>
> *Now, regarding the small successes I mentioned earlier, I learned where your parents live in a small village outside of Venice. Unfortunately the dwindling funds caused me to return to the States. I understand why you may be suspicious of my needing more funds with what one might call a winning hand. I will submit a thorough written report tomorrow at noon.*
>
> *Your Servant,*
> *Walter Chaney*

Rena read and reread his report, which wasn't much different from the verbal comments he'd made the day before. However, being a very smart young lady, she'd asked him to return on this day and bring along the receipts for flights, lodging, and any other large expenses that had contributed to siphoning off the thousands of dollars. The doorbell sounded and she gathered herself together.

"Welcome, Mr. Chaney. Won't you please step on in? We'll go into the small parlor to discuss all the particulars of the trip. I hope you remembered to bring the receipts."

She could tell by the answer he began to give her that he seemed flustered and lost for words, but he suddenly stopped talking when he entered the room and recognized the man standing there.

"Mr. Chaney, let me introduce you to Mr. Hicklin."

"Oh yes, I do know Mr. Hicklin."

"Then you know that Mr. Hicklin is the district attorney of our great city," said Rena.

Mr. Hicklin took charge. He inquired about the receipts, but what he got was a bunch of balderdash.

"I'll ask you just this one time—do you have any receipts?"

Mr. Chaney could no more than turn his head several times to indicate no.

With the answer still floating in the air, Mr. Hicklin opened the front door and motioned for a detective to enter and arrest Mr. Chaney.

Rena sat quietly thinking about the loss of her money, but more disturbing to her was the lack of new information about her parents. She chose this moment to be mature in the face of a huge disappointment. She struggled but managed to hold back her tears. She smiled real big indicating all was well, but inside she was feeling miserable.

Mr. Chaney was handcuffed and led away. He turned and pleaded with her not to press charges, saying that he was desperate for money to care for his family. They were badly in need of doctoring and food.

Rena stood up and asked Mr. Hicklin to please allow Mr. Chaney to explain himself.

After a long adjuration mixed with sniffling and held-back tears, Mr. Chaney dropped his arms, indicating that he had run out of worthy comments to bring mercy on his poor self.

Rena spoke. "Mr. Chaney, I want to ask you why you didn't ask for help." She then turned to Mr. Hicklin. "Is there truth to what this man has said? Or has he stooped so low that he could tell a pathetic made-up story involving a deceased wife and two ailing children?"

Mr. Hicklin bowed his head in a solemn manner and fiddled with his hat in his hands. "His story is true."

Rena slowly rose from her seat and walked over to the window. She stared out for a moment, then turned, took a deep breath, and said, "Mr. Chaney, it's Christmastime, which is not an occasion to imprison a man for taking care of his two sick children, even if it was in a dishonest way. I forgive you, and I will not press charges against you. Mr. Hicklin, please take him away, and thank you for going to all this trouble."

Once the men had left, Rena sat down and cried, not

over the loss of the money but because she had failed at finding her mama and papa. After a short while, she got her emotions under control. She spoke aloud but very softly, "I have a concert next week in a neighboring state, so I need to practice."

And for the next three days, that is all she did—practice, practice, practice.

THE EVENING PERFORMANCE STARTED AT EIGHT, AND Rena was nervous as always. She had taken her place on the piano bench before the Steinway she loved to play. The candles at the maestro's music stand and near the valances on either side of the stage were all lit. She was ready. She awaited the cue, and then the lights in the auditorium dimmed, revealing the candles more prominently.

"Ladies and gentlemen, I have the privilege of introducing the renowned pianist Rena Favro."

The audience rose to their feet to applaud. Rena stood and took a gentle, ladylike bow. Just as she was turning to take her place on the bench, she almost fainted, for she believed she saw her mama and papa—could they really be here from Italy after so many years? No, that seemed impossible.

She sat and played.

AFTER THE CONCERT, RENA WAS IN HER DRESSING ROOM. There was a knock on the door.

Rena said, "Come in."

In walked her mom and dad. When she saw them, she jumped to her feet and went to hug and kiss them and thank them for coming—it wasn't often they showed up at her concerts. As she backed away to look at the two of them, she noticed two other people standing in the open doorway.

She cried, "Mama and Papa!" She would later learn that Mr. Chaney had left behind breadcrumbs—stories and notes with addresses—that Rena's parents were able to use to find Rena's location. Once in the city, they saw her face everywhere on concert posters and ads.

It took what seemed like an eternity for Rena to stop crying, catch her breath, and blot the tears from her face. The questions flew back and forth so fast it was hard to keep up with it all.

At one point, Rena noticed that the Pernells were standing well back, deliberately letting Mama and Papa gather around Rena. Shortly after she noticed this, she asked everyone if she could treat them to a late snack at a nearby café. With one glance shared amongst the group, the decision was unanimous, so off they went.

The discussion was lighthearted until Rena got everyone's attention, indicating she had something of great importance to say.

She said, "I want you to look closely at what is going on here. It is a blessing for sure. How can one person be so blessed? I have my birth parents, Mama and Papa, who brought me into this world, and Mom and Dad, my adoptive parents, who have given me love and support when I was orphaned or lost or perhaps just separated from my Mama and Papa. All I know is it was awful. The problem is that there is no way I can repay you for such unconditional love—it's impossible. All four of you are so selfless. You all cared about my well-being first, and that sort of kindness cannot be repaid."

Not an eye was dry.

And if this wasn't enough, in walked Walter Chaney with his two little children.

He pulled up chairs for the three of them and said, "Please excuse me for butting in. The theater told me where I could find you, Miss Rena. I wanted you to meet my two precious children and see for yourself the outcome of their surgeries. Both were born with calcium deposits under their kneecaps, which required careful scraping and replacing. The limping is gone and now they can even run like the other boys and girls. But they must wear braces for many hours each day. They are happier with themselves and how they look, but what is really magnificent is that the other children don't tease them as before. One last thing and then we must be on our way because it's past their bedtime."

Mr. Chaney pulled an envelope from his pocket and handed it to Rena. "It's all there. Merry Christmas."

Rena was very curious where and how Mr. Chaney came by the money, but the gesture and his heart was so much a part of his kind act that she decided to let it alone. And she remembered, "True living is giving."

Mr. Pernell looked at his wristwatch. "You know, it's getting late. I think this is a good note to end on. 'Good note'—did you catch that, Rena?"

She chuckled. "Yes, Dad, I got that."

Mr. and Mrs. Pernell went around the table and gave Mr. and Mrs. Favro a hug goodbye. And everyone shouted, "Merry Christmas!"

✦

Made in the USA
Columbia, SC
03 June 2021

38749474R00081